Second Chances

Second Chances

ANGELA D. EVANS

authorHOUSE®

AuthorHouse™
1663 Liberty Drive
Bloomington, IN 47403
www.authorhouse.com
Phone: 1-800-839-8640

Published by AuthorHouse 11/03/2014

ISBN: 978-1-4969-5163-2 (sc)
ISBN: 978-1-4969-5164-9 (e)

Library of Congress Control Number: 2014919772

Second Chances

Chapter 1

"Melody get up!

Melody's husband Bill shook her.

"You are the laziest woman I have ever seen. I knew I shouldn't have married you." Melody got up and staggered into the bathroom. "Look at you. You let yourself go. You look old and you're gaining weight. Hurry up I have to get to work."

Melody looked into the bathroom mirror. She began to cry. Her face was badly bruised. She had a black eye. She thought, "What am I going to do. I can't keep going to work like this. If I take off again I might get fired" Melody looked at the clock. She picked up some make up that she had just purchased. It claimed to hide marks. Melody applied some to her face. She moved towards the mirror and looked closely at herself. Melody turned the light on the mirror. She was surprised at the results. Melody quickly put on her clothes. Bill walked over to Melody. He kissed her on the lips. As he walked out of the door he said, "Love you."

Although Melody didn't feel like saying it she said, "Me too."

Melody continued getting dressed. She put on a light jacket because it was a cool morning. She left the house and walked several blocks to catch her bus. Melody was paying a car note, but her husband used it because he worked further away. Her husband Bill had a Lexus that he only drove on special occasions. He didn't want his car to get marks on it and wanted to keep the mileage down. Melody had protested once and they got into a big argument. He had grabbed her in the neck. Bill told her that she was disrespecting him. Bill told Melody that she was the woman and she is to obey her husband.

Whenever Melody would argue the fact he would tell her that she took vows to love, honor and obey.

Melody had walked two blocks before arriving at the bus stop. She waited twenty minutes before the bus arrived. When the bus arrived she got on it. Melody showed her bus pass and then sat down. Melody thought about the night before. She replayed it to try to figure out what had triggered Bill's temper:

"They had come home minutes apart. Bill had gotten off early and had just pulled into the driveway. Melody asked him what he was doing home.

He responded, "Why I can't come home early?"

She responded "That's not what I'm saying. I'm just surprised that you're home this early."

"What you had something planned?"

"No. I'm happy you're home. I'll have someone to eat with."

"Do you want someone home to eat with or someone to put in extra hours and pay the bills and have food for you to eat because your job can't do that? What you want to go out there and find someone? Not with that face. You use to be so beautiful. Now look at you, you're fat. You put on five pounds since we got married. What are you one hundred and ten pounds? You let yourself go. Your face got marks on it. I told you about all that make up. I should trade you in. I didn't think you would get run down so fast. We've only been married three years and you already look run down."

Melody thought, "I didn't say anything, so I don't know why he got so angry. I remember going into the kitchen to start dinner and that's when he came up behind me and punched me in the eye. I was just about to turn. That's why the bruise is where it is. I stopped saying anything and he still hits me. I don't know what I am supposed to do. Then he wants me to still cook and wonders why it's taking me some time. All during dinner he's still yelling at me and talking how bad a person I am. I just sat there. We ate dinner. He complained about how slow I was eating. I couldn't believe he wanted to have sex after I came up from cleaning the kitchen. He told me to clean up, which meant take a shower and put on perfume and a night gown. I do as I'm told. I layed down and when he touched me I was fidgety. I didn't want to have sex. I was hurt and angry. He kissed me. After a while I returned his kisses and then his passion. Tears filled my eyes. I hated how he could make me feel so good when I wanted to hate him."

The buzzer rang and jarred Melody's mind back to the present. Melody looked out of the window. She was a block away from her stop. When the bus pulled off Melody pushed the buzzer.

After getting off the bus she walked three blocks. When she walked into the office everyone looked at her. She knew they talked about her coming in with bruises. She could feel them look her over. Melody walked over to her seat and sat down. She was happy that they couldn't see through her makeup this time. Melody got her things together and then went to court. She set up her computer and waited for the judge to begin.

Melody's mind drifted off:

Melody thought of when she and Bill first met. He was a kind man. On their first date Bill took her to a Spanish restaurant. He opened the door for her. He was very romantic. On their second date Bill got angry at the guy who parked his car. Bill said that the man scratched his car. They almost got into a fight. Melody shrugged that off. Melody just thought it was one time. After they had dated a year Bill proposed. He had a beautiful ring. It showed that he had thought about it.

The sheriff's officer came into the court room and Melody's day began. As she went through her day Melody's mind was focused on her life. She did everything mechanically. She had done her work so often that it didn't require much thought.

By lunch time she was hungry. Melody hadn't eaten very much. She tried not to eat a lot around Bill because he always commented on her weight.

Melody thought about her life with Bill: *"For the first year of their lives together Bill was great. He complimented her on a regular basis. Bill often stated that he loved the way her body felt next to his. There were occasions that he lost his temper and then apologized. He never hit her then. The first time that he really lost it was their first year anniversary. The waiter messed up the order. When she tried to talk to Bill about it he grabbed her arm. He told her after he had calmed down to never question him. He apologized for loosing his temper with her. After that he was very attentive. Six months later Melody told him that she was pregnant. He snapped saying, "Did we talk about this? What you want to be the man?" Melody didn't know what to do, so she tried to do whatever he said and how he said to do it. She ended up getting an abortion because he told her that he didn't say that he wanted one then."*

When lunch was over Melody returned to the court room. When the judge came on the bench again Melody turned on the tape. She listened as a woman told the judge why she was seeking a divorce. Melody listened as the woman told the judge through tears soaked eyes everything that she was feeling about Bill. Melody listened intently to every word. After the woman had gone Melody thought about her own life: *She had been married for three years now. The second anniversary it started out romantic and then turned to him abusing her. Their third anniversary Bill bought her flowers. Something that was sprayed on the flowers made Melody sneeze. Bill was offended and threw the flowers in the outside trash. He cancelled their reservation saying, "That may set off that annoying sneezing." They stayed home and Melody cooked. She tried to make it romantic, but for Bill it was over. When they went to bed Melody wore lingerie that she had purchased for the night. Melody thought that she looked good in it.*

She had been working out. Although she was thin, Melody had a nice shape. Her body was proportioned. Melody was five feet and nine inches, one hundred and ten pounds and very curvy. She had long hair that she kept straight except for a flip at the end. Her hair was always in place and she dressed well. She had a model's walk and attracted many men because of it. Melody had a pleasant personality and was liked right off by most of the people who came in contact with her. She didn't wear much make up except on the occasion that Bill hit her somewhere visible. *That night Melody walked over to Bills side of the bed. Although he had his eyes closed he had not fallen asleep. She kissed him lightly on the lips. When she saw that he was receptive she sat on the bed. She kissed him more passionately. Bill wrapped his hands around her waist. After kissing for a while Bill pulled her onto the bed. He kissed her passionately. Melody felt like she had when Bill was kind to her. They made love into the night. The next morning Bill got up early, showered and went down to the den. Melody laid awake thinking about the night. She wrapped her arms around her body thinking of how good she felt. Bill came into the room. He said, "What are you doing? What I wasn't enough for you last night?" Melody tried to explain, but Bill told her that he didn't want to hear it and to get up and cook breakfast. On his way out of the room he called her fat and lazy.*

"Melody!"

She didn't answer.

"Melody."

Melody jumped. She was brought back to the present.

"I'm sorry. I didn't hear you come up."

"I noticed that you were deep in thought. Are you alright?"

"I'm fine. How are you?'

"I'm better now that I've spoken to you. Hey do me a favor go to the lady's room and touch that up."

"What?"

Juan motioned to her eye.

"Excuse me."

When Melody returned Juan was still there.

"Are you alright?"

"Yes. I'm fine. Thank you."

"You know if you ever need anything or anyone I'm here. You are too beautiful a woman for anyone to do that to you."

"Thank you. It's nothing."

"Remember if you need a shoulder (Juan winked at her) or anything else I am here."

"I know. Thank you."

Juan walked off. Melody thought about what he said and what he's always saying. She wondered if he was true to his word. She thought about all the comments that he's made and all the hurtful things that Bill has said. "How can one man think that I'm ugly and fat and another constantly tells me how beautiful I am?"

After work Melody walked to the bus stop. Melody thought of what both men said. As Melody walked passed a building with a mirror she looked at herself. She heard a car horn. Melody looked back. It was Juan.

"Hey beautiful. Would you like a ride?"

Melody was tired and wanted to get home. She thought it safe since Bill usually gets home late. She walked over to the car.

"Sure."

Juan opened the door from inside of the car. Melody got into the car.

"Woman you are gorgeous. If that man isn't appreciating you I can take care of that." (Juan looked down at Melody's thighs and licked his lips.)

"Juan you know you talk a lot of stuff."

Juan smiled.

"And I can back up every word. Why don't you try me out?"

"We shouldn't be talking like this. I'm married and I'm sure there's someone in your life."

"I know you're married, but (Juan smoothed his hand over her face) he's not taking care of you like he should. I would never put my hands on you to harm you. Besides I'm not attached."

"I can't believe that."

"Believe it. I'm waiting for you."

"Stop flirting."

"I'm for real. You need to dump that joker."

"I love him Juan."

"How, when he does this?" (Juan touched her eye with gentleness.)

"He wasn't always like this. He was very kind and gentle."

"But is he taking care of business?"

"Why do you think that you can ask me that?"

"I didn't mean to offend. It's just that when I want something I go all out."

"But you know that I'm married."

"Yes I do, but he's not treating you right."

"I never said that."

"It's obvious. You have makeup on today."

"I wear makeup sometimes."

"Not like this. For the most part you only have lip stick sometimes. Most of the time you are naturally beautiful. The only time that you wear what you have on is when your husband has hit you."

"Thank you for the compliment, but how do you know this?"

"I'm attracted to you. I notice everything about you."

"You're serious."

"Yes I am. Just say the word. You can stay with me."

"Thank you, but I'll be fine."

"If you ever need to get away just call; I'll come get you. Here's my address."

"No, that's okay. If my husband finds this he'll really go off."

"You need to be able to reach me. At least look at the address so if you can't call me you can get there."

To humor Juan Melody looked at the address.

"I can't take a bus here."

Juan looked at her surprised.

"I mean if I even thought of leaving, there isn't a bus line that goes there."

"Well memorize the number. I'll be wherever you call me from."

"Well I better get out of this car."

"Fine. Promise me you'll call if you need someone."

With hesitation Melody said, "I promise."

Chapter 2

She had Juan drop her off around the corner of her house. Melody stepped out of the car. When she reached her house Melody noticed that her car was out front. She became nervous. She looked at her watch. She was a little early. Melody figured that she'll say that the bus was early.

When Melody walked into the house it was dark. After Melody closed the door she felt something hit her on the side of her face. She stumbled. Melody tried to collect herself and then she felt something chocking her. She tried to pull it from her neck, but the grip was too strong. She felt herself loosing consciousness. As she was about to pass out Melody found herself being released and she fell to the floor. Melody could barely make out what was going on. She saw two figures and then Melody passed out.

When Melody awakened she was in the hospital. She looked around. When she went to get up Juan woke up and stopped her.

"What are you doing here? What am I doing here?"

"After you got out of the car I followed you. It didn't feel right, when you left. When I pulled up in front of your house I saw that it was dark. I saw a window curtain slightly open. I saw it move and then a body almost fall. I knocked on the door and heard a man yelling. I tried the handle. The door was locked. I forced the door open. When I came in I saw a man which turned out to be your husband with an extension cord around your neck. I forced him to release you."

Melody just stared at Juan. She closed her eyes briefly. When she opened them back up tears were in her eyes.

"Where's Bill?"

Juan stared at Melody for a second with a cold expression. Then his expression softened.

"He's in jail. I called the police after I got him down. I talked to them. You don't have to press charges. They did that. They did tell me that it is in your best interest to get a restraining order."

"I can't think about that right now."

14

"No ones' going to rush you. Do you have somewhere to go?"

"No. I don't have any friends and my family lives far and besides we're not close."

"You can stay with me."

"Do you think that's wise?"

"Do you want to go to a shelter?"

Tears streamed down Melody's face.

"No."

"Then come home with me. I won't pressure you for anything. You won't owe me. I just want to help you."

"I appreciate all of your help."

"We're friends right?"

"You have been a good one."

Melody was released the next day. Juan was there to pick her up. When they arrived at Juan's home Melody was surprised. The house was a one family home with two stories. It had a two car garage that led into the house. The kitchen was large and opened into the living and dinning room. It was clean, but showed signs of being lived in. Upstairs was the master bedroom and two other bedrooms with bathrooms adjoined. Melody was set up in one of the guest rooms. She took a shower and laid down. Melody slept several hours before she heard a knock on the door. She was still foggy.

"Come in." (Juan didn't hear her, so he knocked again) Melody said a little louder, "Come in."

Juan came into the room.

"Are you alright?"

"Yes. I'm okay."

"You don't sound too good."

"I'm alright. I'm just tired from all of the medicine."

"Are you hungry?"

"Oh I forgot to call the job."

"Don't worry. I told them that you had an accident and would be out a while."

"Thank you so much."

"No problem."

"I'm going to bring you up some soup. It'll be easier for you. What kind of soup do you like?"

"You don't have to do that."

"I know I don't. I want to. You need someone to take care of you right now. I'm here. Let me take care of you."

Tears formed in Melody's eyes. Juan walked over to the bed. He sat down and put his arm around her shoulders. Melody laid her head on his chest. He caressed her hair.

After Melody gained her composure Juan went down to the kitchen and prepared soup.

When it was ready Juan took it upstairs. He knocked on Melody's room door. She told him to come in. He placed a tray in her lap and then the soup. Juan sat quietly while Melody ate.

After Melody was finished she thanked him.

"I must have been hungrier than I thought."

"That's good you have an appetite. You could stand to gain a little weight. Not that you're not gorgeous, because you are."

Melody tried to smile.

"What am I going to do? Everything is in his name. My money goes into a joint account with Bills'."

Juan looked at her in disbelief.

"I'm not trying to push this, but you may want to get that restraining order."

"I know I sound pitiful, but I took my vows serious and I let the man be the man."

"Having your own doesn't take anything from the man."

"Can you take me to the bank?"

"When would you like to go?"

"Today."

"Are you up to it?"

"I have to be. I need money and to stop by my house."

"No problem. Last I checked he's still locked up."

Melody took a shower and used the toothbrush from the hospital. Melody put back on the clothes that she was wearing. The two left Juan's home and headed to her house. The police had fixed the door where no one could get in. Melody went around the back of the house and opened the back door.

When they entered the house Melody took all of her important paperwork and then packed a suitcase. Juan placed the suitcase in the back of the car and then they left for the bank. When they entered the bank Juan went with her to talk with the bank representative. The representative stared at Melody. Juan cleared his throat. The representative excused herself. She shifted her eyes to the computer. The woman saw that Melody and Bill had a joint account and that nothing was in it. She informed Melody of this. Melody stared at the representative. Melody explained that all of her money was put into the account and that she had not used any of it. The woman divulged that there was another account, but Melody's name was not on it. Melody put her head in her hands. As if talking to the table under her Melody asked, "What am I going to do?" The representative felt bad for Melody. She had been in an abusive relationship herself and knew the signs. As far as Melody was concerned one didn't have to know the signs, for she had bruises to her face and there was a scar around her neck from where Bill had choked her with the extension cord.

Already knowing the answer the representative asked, "Is your husband available to authorize money transfer?"

Still with her head down Melody answered, "No."

"Wait here, I'll talk with my supervisor and see if I can get approval for the transaction." The representative excused herself and then went to talk to her supervisor. When the representative returned she was smiling. Mrs. Turner I was given authorization to transfer $10,000.00, into your joint account. You can than sign a withdrawal slip or transfer it into another account that will just be in your name. Personally between you and me I would cash out the check and take the cash. Just until you get things settled." Melody looked at her with mixed emotions. "I understand. We sisters have to stick together." The woman finished processing the transaction. "Look if you need anymore money you will be able to get additional funds in a week."

"I have direct deposit. How do I stop it?"

"I can close out the account today. You can tell your job to stop it immediately. I'll tell you what if you're expecting money call and ask for me (the woman handed Melody her business card.) and I'll check your account. If it's here come back and cash it out."

"Thank you so much. I don't know what I would have done without your help."

After Melody and Juan left, he asked, "What does she mean by sister, she's white?"

"She meant sisters through domestic violence."

Juan looked at her with a questioning expression on his face.

Melody said, "She is what you call a survivor of domestic violence."

"That woman, she looks good."

"Well I don't know how long it's been, but when you're not getting beat down, not just physical, that's what you look like. I'm happy that I got her. With this money I can get my own place."

"Don't rush into anything. You can stay with me for as long as you want or need to."

Melody leaned over and kissed Juan on the cheek. "Thank you."

The two returned to Juan's home. They ordered takeout and had the food delivered. They talked throughout the night. Melody enjoyed Juan's conversation. He was warm and understanding. She felt secure and not worried that something she say may set him off. Juan called the job on Monday and took the week off to help Melody get situated. Melody was able to retrieve her car. She got the number and name of the officer who arrested Bill. Everyday for the next month Melody called the officer. She was always told the same thing; that Bill was still being held and they didn't have any further information.

Second Chances

Chapter 3

Another month went by and Melody decided that it was time for her to get her own place. Juan tried to encourage Melody to get a restraining order, but she refused, instead Melody searching for a place to live.................................

Two weeks into looking for a place a police officer called Juan's house. Melody heard the phone ring, but did not answer it. Juan told her that he did not mind, but she didn't feel comfortable doing it. Juan picked up the phone. He said hello. After a few minutes he handed the phone to Melody. She took the phone and spoke to the person on the phone. She listened intently. A worried look came over her face.

After she hung up Juan went over to Melody and held her.

"He got released?"

"Yes."

"Just like that?"

"He has a no contact order and a return to court scheduled in a month, where I will be subpoenaed to appear."

"Are you sure you want to leave now?"

"I can't hide out here forever. Besides if he knows that I'm living here it'll only make it worst."

"I can handle it."

"I don't want any trouble, for you or me. You shouldn't have to deal with anything like this."

"What if he finds where you moved? At least if you're here I can protect you."

"I have to learn to be by myself."

"But you don't have to be alone."

"Thank you for all of your help, but I have to do this for me."

"Okay I won't push."

Bill called Melody's cell phone. She told him that she couldn't talk to him because of the court order.

Melody found an apartment two weeks later. Bill continued to call Melody's cell phone. She put it on do not answer.

Juan helped Melody move what few things she had into her apartment.

When they arrived at Melody's apartment, they carried a few things up with them. Melody's car alarm went off. She clicked it off and continued placing her boxes down. The alarm went off again. Melody clicked it off again.

"I wonder......."

She stopped in mid stream.

"What were you about to say?"

"I was going to say I wonder if the car did this when Bill had it. I think somehow Bill followed us and he's outside."

They both walked to the window. They didn't see anyone outside. There were more boxes in the car, but Melody was afraid to go outside.

"Maybe you should call the police."

"And say what? My husband is making my alarm go off."

"Well I'll go out to my car and get boxes out. You stay inside and watch for him."

"I'm afraid of you going out as well."

"We can't stay up here. We have to do something."

"I know, but I don't want you to get involved."

"I'm already involved. I care for you."

Melody looked at Juan with sadness in her eyes.

"I'm sorry."

"Sorry for what?"

"You care about me and I have all of this going on."

"There's nothing for you to be sorry about. You didn't ask for all of this mess and you didn't ask me to care about you."

Juan cupped her face and lightly kissed Melody on the nose. I'll be back. Melody watched as Juan walked out the door. Melody went over to the window to make sure that Juan was alright. Juan gathered a few boxes and then returned to the building. When he got to Melody's door she had opened it. Juan walked into the apartment and Melody closed it behind them. She made sure that the door was locked.

"So I guess it was a false alarm."

"I don't think so. I think he didn't come out because you came down."

"You think so?"

"I'm sure he remembers you."

"Then you should stay up here and I'll bring everything up."

"I hate for you to do all of this by yourself."

"Don't worry about it. I don't mind."

Juan moved all of Melody's things out of his car. Melody gave Juan her car keys. He moved all of her things out of her car.

When he had completed the task Melody offered to order take-out for the two of them. Juan accepted partly because he wanted to spend time with her and he also wanted to protect her from Bill.....................

When the food came Juan answered the door. He paid the delivery person and took the food. Juan locked the door back. Melody laid cloth on the floor. She and Juan ate. They talked throughout the meal. Melody even managed to laugh a couple of times. Juan knew that she was afraid and that Melody would try to be brave and stay in her apartment alone.

"Melody it's getting late. I know you won't ask and I know you are trying to be brave, but I would like to stay with you tonight. Don't argue with me. I don't feel comfortable leaving you alone tonight."

Melody smiled. She got up from the floor and got the blow up mattress. Juan assisted her. When they had gotten the mattress blown up Juan assisted her in making up the bed. Melody laid on one side and Juan on the other. They said good night.

After a half hour of both of them having trouble falling asleep Juan heard a sniffle. Juan turned toward Melody. He could not see her face. He moved closer to Melody and placed his arms around her. He held her close.

Through a muffled voice Juan heard Melody ask, "Am I a bad person?"

Juan took his hand and turned her face to him.

"No you're not. You are an incredible woman. You're beautiful, smart and any man would be lucky to have you."

With tears filled eyes Melody closed them. Tears rolled down her face. Juan kissed her wet face. She turned to face Juan.

"I tried to be the wife that he wanted. I kept our house clean. I tried not to argue or talk back to him. No matter what I did I couldn't seem to please him."

"Don't put his hang ups onto yourself. It's him who has the problem, not you."

"I've been with him so long. I've only been with him."

Juan looked at her.

"He was your first love?"

"Yes and only."

"Listen you know they say that some people are in your life for a reason and some for a season. I don't know what reason you ended up with him, maybe so when you meet the real Mr. Right you will appreciate him. But as far as the season, he was your Spring."

Melody laid her head on his chest. Juan laid back. He continued to hold Melody and they fell asleep...................................……....

Several hours later the alarm went off on her car. Melody jumped. Juan felt her and awakened.

"What's wrong?"

"The alarm on my car."

"Let it go off. Someone will make a complaint. If the police come they will run a check and then come to this apartment. Then you can tell them what you suspect and that he's been calling you."

"You think that will stop him?"

"If he is out there and they catch him, he might get locked back up and additional charges may be added."

"I hate to think of him going to jail. I hate to think of anyone going to jail. You know he's never been in trouble."

"Are you his first girlfriend, his first?"

Melody looked at Juan.

"No. He had other girlfriends. If you're asking me if I was his first sexual encounter the answer is no. He was very popular. He was two years older than me. I thought I was something dating an upper classman."

Melody smiled as she thought of it.

"How long did you date before you got married?"

"We dated three years. We got married a year after I finished school. He wanted to get married sooner, but my parents wouldn't let me marry before I finished school."

"Why did he rush it?"

"Well he felt that we've been together a long time and he wanted to make love to me." (Melody looked down) He wanted me to be pure on our wedding night. So he would barely kiss me. He didn't want us to be tempted and he said that it was hard."

"I agree with him on that."

Melody looked curiously at Juan.

"What do you mean by that?"

31

"I know you've been distracted with all that's been going on in your life. Haven't you even thought about us? I'm sorry. That wasn't fare."

Melody looked at Juan with compassion.

"I'm sorry that I've been so absorbed in my world of madness."

"You don't have to apologize. It was unfair of me to even consider that you would have feelings for anyone other than your husband. I don't mean to disrespect you or your husband. I care a lot about you and I'm willing to wait for when you're ready. That's if you are even interested in me."

Melody stood for a few minutes looking at Juan. She thought about what he said. She smoothed her hand over his face.

"Juan I don't know if I can say that I'm interested in you right now. Yes I see how handsome you are. I see how good a person you are. I appreciate how good you have been to me. I do care for you. I can't tell you in what since, but know that you have a place in my heart. I can't do better than that right now. Know that I don't want you to go away."

"Fair enough."

Juan put his hand out. Melody took it. Juan pulled her to him. When Melody didn't resist Juan pulled the hand that he held and put it around his waist. He put his free hand around her waist and gently pulled her closer. Melody placed her head on his chest. He let go of her hand and placed his other hand around her back. Melody's arm remained behind his back and she placed her other hand on his arm. They stayed locked in this position until a knock on the door interrupted them. Melody stayed frozen. Juan took his arms from around her and walked over to the door. Juan looked through the peep hole and as he opened the door looked back and said that it was the police. Melody walked to the door.

"Is there a Mrs. Turner here?"

"Yes officer, I am Mrs. Turner."

The officer read the license plate number, "Is this your vehicle?"

"Yes officer."

"Do you know it's been going off for some time now? One of your neighbors called the prescient complaining about the noise."

"Officer please come in. I would like to speak to you about something."

Melody moved back and the officer entered the apartment. He looked around.

"Are you just moving in, or moving out?"

"I actually just moved in earlier today."

"You know this is a nice neighborhood and you don't want to make your neighbors not want you here."

"Officer I am not trying to be a nuisance. My husband. (The officer looked at Juan and made a curious expression.) This is my friend Juan Mattos."

"You did say your husband right?"

"Yes. He assaulted me a few weeks ago. Mr. Mattos saved my life. My husband was released from jail a week ago. He has been calling me on my cell phone. I asked him to stop. (Tears formed in Melody's eyes. Juan instinctively came to Melody's side and put his arm around her to comfort her.) The court gave him a no contact order. They filed a criminal complaint against him. He has a court date coming up. What I was about to say earlier was that my car alarm has been going off several times today. I think that my husband has followed me here and is triggering the alarm."

"Have you seen him?"

"No, but before today my alarm did not go off every few minutes. There aren't any people around, not much traffic and the wind is calm."

"I'm sorry Mrs. Turner (He looked at Juan when he said Mrs.) there is nothing that I can do, because you have only a suspicion. No real proof. I tell you what, I will circle the block a couple of times to see if I spot anyone on the street."

"Thank you very much officer."

"Just make sure you keep the noise down." (Again he looked at Juan when he made the statement) Mr. Mattos are you staying here tonight?"

"Yes."

The officer looked at Juan with a raised eyebrow.

"Mrs. Turner I'll let you know if I see anything. Take care and call the precinct if your husband shows up."

"I will."

The officer left.

Melody said, "Did you see how he reacted when I said my husband and the expression that he gave you?"

"Don't worry about it."

"Am I doing something wrong?"

"No. I am your friend and will remain it. You don't need to be alone right now."

Melody walked over to Juan, placed both hands on the side of his face and lightly kissed him on his lips. "Thank you." She took him by the hand and led him over to the mattress. "We better get some sleep."

The two laid down both facing each other but not touching. Melody closed her eyes. Juan watched her. She soon drifted off to sleep. He watched her breathe in and out. Juan thought how peaceful she looked. He wanted to pull her to him, caress and make love to her. Juan wanted to assure her that she would be safe with him, but he held back. He didn't want to rush her into anything that she wasn't ready for and most of all scare her away..........

After several hours of watching and longing for her he got up. There wasn't any furniture, so Juan sat on the radiator in the kitchen. He looked out of the window into the darkness. A couple of times Juan thought he saw something and it proved to be nothing. Towards dawn Juan returned to the mattress. He laid down cautiously trying not to wake Melody. He drifted off to sleep.

Melody was dreaming: *She was in a house. She recognized it to be Juan's. Melody walked upstairs to the master bedroom. Juan was taking off his suit. He said, "Hey you're home early."*

Melody asked, "What do you mean?"

Juan walked over to her and asked, "What's wrong?"

"What are you doing here?"

"Did you forget our wedding already? We've been married for six months." Melody looked confused. Juan lifted her left hand and showed her the wedding ring. She noticed that it was different. "See this is the wedding ring that I bought for you last year." Juan put his arms around her waist and kissed her. "Have you forgotten this?" He kissed her several times. "Bill is in jail. You divorced him right after so we could be together." Juan kissed her neck. She relaxed. He pulled her closer, with one hand pressed against her back and the other on her waist. Melody's arms remained by her side. Juan continued to kiss Melody until she returned his affections. After they had kissed for some time Juan moved to kissing her neck.

She heard her name being called and she woke up. Melody was surprised to find herself underneath Juan. He was looking down at her. Melody looked at Juan in a questioning manner.

Juan said, "I thought that I was dreaming, but when it got this good I woke up." Melody looked embarrassed. Juan cupped her face. "Hey don't look like that. Look we still have our clothes on. No harm done."

"I thought that I was dreaming. I didn't realize."

"I guess we both were having some powerful dreams."

"I can't believe. I've never."

Juan smiled down at her. "Well I guess you are more attracted to me than you thought. Don't worry yourself about it. We didn't make love."

"Yeah, but if you hadn't awakened and if you hadn't stopped."

"Yeah, well I want you fully aware when, I mean if we get together. Juan realized that she was still halfway under him. "Oh excuse me." Juan moved off of Melody. She moved over. Juan glanced over at the window. "Hey it looks like a beautiful day out there. Let's drive down the shore and take in the sites?"

"I still have to get my apartment together. I don't have any furniture."

"Well I'll tell you what, come home with me so I can change clothes. Then I'll take you to look for furniture."

"You don't have to do that. I'll be alright."

"I know I don't have to. I want to."

"Ok. Let me get dressed and I'll be ready."

While Melody dressed Juan went over to the kitchen window and looked out of it. He looked over towards Melody's car. Everything looked fine. He thought to himself, "I guess having the police come by and circling the block did the trick." Melody walked into the kitchen. Juan turned around. Melody blushed from the expression on Juan's face.

"Woman you look good."

"Thank you. I'm ready."

Juan thought to himself, "I wish."

Melody and Juan left her apartment. She checked her door to make sure it was locked. They got into Juan's car. As Juan drove off

Melody surveyed the area. Juan noticed and placed his hand over hers.

"Everything is going to be okay."

"I hope so."

"You have to have faith."

"I do. I've prayed continuously for things to get better."

"Well maybe this is the way it has to happen for you to move on to what God has planned for you."

"I thought Bill was for me."

"At that time, but now it's time for you to move on. Some people you aren't suppose to spend a life time with."

"I figured when you get married that's it. I don't understand. You are suppose to only get married once, that is for life."

"Well if the person treats you right. There are times that are acceptable for you to get out of a marriage and I think your situation meets it more than enough."

Melody was quiet the remainder of the ride............................

When they arrived at his home Juan parked. He got out of the car and walked over to the passenger side. Juan opened the door. He held his hand out and she took it. He quickly let it go in case Bill had followed them. The two entered his home. "If you're hungry fix something while I'm dressing. I'm just going to take a quick shower. It won't take me very long."

Melody was feeling a little hungry. She had not eaten since dinner and it had been a long night. Melody knew her way around the kitchen. Melody cooked scrambled eggs with peppers, onions and tomatoes. She toast some bread and made a pot of coffee. When Juan entered the kitchen he was surprised.

"Wow you cooked?"

"Yes. What, you thought I couldn't cook?"

"I didn't know. Is it good?"

"Yes. Sit down."

Melody fixed his plate.

"Wow, a man could get use to this." He waited until she had fixed her plate and sat down. Juan said grace and they began to eat. "Wow, this is good. Woman if I knew that you cooked like this I would have asked you to cook for me on a regular. Can you cook more than eggs this good?"

"Yes I can."

"Well look I think I'll be visiting you at dinner time."

Melody looked at him and smiled. He noticed that the same sentiment wasn't in her eyes. In her eyes he saw sadness. "I didn't mean to make you sad."

"You didn't. It's just that after so many years of being with a person to think of not being with them, even when they're not good for you."

Juan looked at Melody and he thought of what she said. He was happy to hear her say that Melody knew that she needed to let Bill go.

"I know. You are a strong woman and you will get through this."

The two finished eating. They shared in cleaning the kitchen.

Juan said, "This is nice. I've never shared cleaning the kitchen with anyone."

Melody looked at him.

"You've never did dishes with anyone?"

"No. My mother is old school. She waits on my father. I wouldn't expect that from my wife." (He nudged Melody) I would like you to be my wife." (Melody looked at him in amazement) "No pressure."

"How do you know that you want me for your wife?"

"I've been interested in you since you came to work. I was told that you were married, so I didn't approach you. Only when I saw the change in you, I knew that something was going on in your marriage. Then I noticed you calling out, showing up late and trying to cover up bruises. You went from wearing no makeup to wearing a lot of it, but it didn't really look like you." (Melody looked embarrassed. Juan faced her and held both arms) "I didn't mean to make you feel bad. I meant that you are so beautiful you don't need anything."

"Why me?"

"You don't choose who you fall in love with." Melody looked at Juan in disbelief. "It's true. Don't think that I'm trying to run a line. I wasn't trying to disrespect your marriage, that's why I haven't said anything before now. I won't try to rush you. All I ask is for you to give me a chance when you're ready."

"I'm still married."

"Only on paper. When your husband hit you he violated your vows." (Melody gave him a strange look) "He vowed to love, but in a twisted sort of way. Honor and cherish, well he broke that vow when he started beating and putting you down. I'm not telling you to do anything that would make you feel bad. I'm just saying that you are not wrong if you're feeling anything for me."

"I think we better go."

"Okay. As you wish."

The two were quiet until they arrived at the furniture store. Juan parked the car. They got out and when the two entered the store one of the sales people came up to them. He asked were they newlyweds. Juan told the guy that he was working on it. The salesman told Juan to buy Melody something pretty and he would win her over. They walked around the store. Melody picked a few items and asked them to deliver it. There was an available date on Tuesday.

After Juan and Melody left the furniture store she wanted to go shopping for dishes. Juan took her to a department store. Melody was able to find dishes, silverware and other household items. Melody and Juan decided to eat out before returning to her apartment..............

When they arrived at her apartment the door was open. Juan went in first. They looked around, but nothing was touched. Melody didn't call the police. She feared that they would think that she was trying to trump up charges on Bill. Juan volunteered to stay. Melody tried to put on a brave face and say that she would be alright. Juan gave her an ultimatum. He told her that either he stay the night at her place or she go to his house. He refused to leave her. Juan and Melody sat on the radiator in the kitchen and looked out the window. She began to cry. Juan put his arm around her shoulders. She laid her head on his chest.

"Everything is going to be alright."

"When? I don't know why he is doing this to me. I don't know why he did the mean things that he did."

Juan could see that Melody was getting angry.

"Don't let your husband change who you are."

Melody looked at him curiously. Then he saw the expression on her face change. She kissed him. "What was that for?"

She kissed him again. This time with passion. He held her face with both of his hands. They sat in the window kissing. As the kiss continued Juan's hands moved to Melody's shoulders. He squeezed them. Melody and Juan continued kissing. He wrapped his arms around her and held her. She stopped kissing him and then laid her head on his chest again. He held her.

Chapter 4

Melody said softly, "Juan make love to me."

It was so soft that he wasn't sure he heard right. He took his hands from around her. He pulled her from him to look at her. He tried to read her expression. She kissed him. He returned the kiss. Juan cupped her chin and said, "What are you trying to do to me?"

She got up and took him by the hand. He got up and followed her.

Juan asked, "What are you doing?" While still holding Juan's hand Melody sat on the inflatable mattress. "Are you sure?"

"Juan please."

Juan sat down next to her. He saw sadness in her eyes. "Are you sure? I don't want to complicate things."

Melody expression changed. Juan saw sincerity. "My life has been complicated for a long time. Juan I want to feel pleasure again. You've been wanting me for a long time and I'm happy you did. Now I want you. I want you to make me feel again. I want to feel love. Can you do that for me?"

Juan looked into her eyes and saw truth. He cupped her chin and kissed her. He smoothed his hand down the side of her face and down her neck. He nibbled her ear lobe. Tears rolled down her face. Juan kissed them. He kissed each eye. She held his head. He kissed her passionately. Juan removed his shirt and then hers. He looked at her. She could see the desire in his eyes. He smoothed the back of his hand down the middle of her breast. Melody shivered. She watched his every move. Juan kissed every place that he touched. The desire that she saw in his eyes brought her to a place she had never been. Juan's desire took them to a place where logic no longer had a place. Melody no longer knew this man. She let go and a woman she had not known took over. Melody took over and Juan enjoyed this side of her. Juan took Melody into his arms again and kissed her until her mind reeled. Their bodies fit each others as if meant to be together. Their pleasures heightened until their bodies could take no more. Juan and Melody held onto each other, tightly and then collapsed out of exhaustion. Juan smiled at Melody, kissed her and she continued to lay in his arms. They closed their eyes and then drifted off to sleep...............................

Juan awakened. He smiled when he looked down and Melody was in his arms. Her arms were still around him as well. Juan kissed her hair. Melody continued sleeping. She stirred once. Juan laid there holding Melody, wanting to provide her with warmth and security. He wanted to give her all the things that Bill failed at. Juan thought about their night together. He wondered if Melody would have any regrets when she awakened. Juan recalled how she had touched and kissed him. He always imagined how Melody would be in bed, but never dreamed she would be the way she was last night. She had let go and went with what felt good.

As he thought about their love making Juan became aroused. He tried to fight it, but here he was laying naked beside the only woman he had truly loved and she was also unclothed. He wanted to repeat the things that they had done the night before. Juan wanted to feel the pleasure that he had felt with this woman. He felt like a virgin who had their very first sexual experience. He had felt pleasure in the past, but nothing such as this. He let his guard down and was driven to feel that pleasure again. Juan began to caress Melody's body. He kissed her lips. Although she returned his kiss she remained asleep. Juan continued to caress Melody's body. He kissed her breast and caressed them. Juan moved down her body. He heard Melody moan. After some time of him kissing and caressing Melody's body she awakened, still in a dream state. She caressed his hair. Melody smoothed her hand down his face. He looked up at her. Her eyes were partly opened. Juan thought she looked more beautiful. She pulled him up by his shoulders and they kissed. Juan found her passion to match the night before and they were lost in their pleasure..............................

When they awakened several hours later Juan got up and held his hand out to Melody. She took it and got up. They walked into the bathroom and got into the shower together. Juan and Melody took turns washing each other. They took their time lost in their own world. Neither thought outside of the pleasure that they were feeling in this intimate setting.

When they were done each took turns drying the other off.

After dressing Melody went into the kitchen and began cooking breakfast. Although it was late in the afternoon she had a taste for breakfast.

"Juan."

"Yes." He walked into the kitchen.

"I didn't ask, but are you in for breakfast. I just have a taste for it."

He walked over to Melody and kissed her on the nose. "I want whatever you're cooking."

She smiled shyly. Juan thought to himself, "How can a woman who resembles such shyness be the way she is in bed?"

"When we're finished eating I need to go home and change clothes. Do you want to come with?"

"Juan I have to stay here alone eventually. I'm grateful for you wanting to protect me, but you had a life before all of this and I don't want to take you from that."

"Woman have you not been listening? I want you to be my life. I enjoy being with you" Juan was quiet for a few minutes. His expression changed. "Am I smothering you? Do you have regrets about last night?"

Melody stopped what she was doing and walked over to Juan. She took him by the hand and led him into the kitchen. She walked over to the stove, picked up a plate and handed it to him. She made herself a plate and then sat down next to him on the radiator. She put a spoonful of food in her mouth. When she was finished chewing Melody placed her plate on the stove. She then took Juan's and did the same thing. She took both of his hands in hers.

"Last night was wonderful." She looked shyly at him. "I had never done any of those things before last night. I've seen some of those things done in movies." She looked up. Juan gave her a surprised look. "Really. Bill wasn't into doing a lot. He wasn't bad,

(Melody looked down again) but nothing like you." Juan smiled. "No I don't have any regrets and I do want this relationship. I'm going to take off Monday and get paperwork to file for a divorce." Juan again looked surprised. "I shouldn't have any problems getting it signed by the judge, do to the circumstances." Juan continued to look at Melody in disbelief. He was amazed and happy at her words. Melody reached over and kissed Juan on the lips. She released his hands and then got up. She picked up his plate and handed it to him and then she got her food. They did not say another word. They ate in quiet and each were comforted by Melody's words..........................

When Monday came Melody got up early. She called into work. She then dressed and started her day..

By the end of the day some of her furniture had been delivered and she had completed her papers for divorce. She certified them and had messenger deliver a copy to Bill.

Melody was comforted when a month had gone by and she had not heard anything from Bill. She and Juan had gone out on several dates. Juan had not stayed the night since their sexual encounter and they had not had sex since. Melody was proud of herself for staying alone in her apartment. She had not returned to Juan's house either. Juan would pick her up for a date or they would talk at work, keeping it casual or on the phone. Melody was happy that they were taking it slow.

Second Chances

Chapter 5

Two months had passed Melody was returning home from work. She picked up the mail and entered her apartment. Melody sorted through the mail. In the mail were two letters. One letter was from court noticing her that her divorce hearing had been scheduled. The second letter was from criminal court noticing her that she was scheduled to appear in court to give testimony concerning Bill's case. Her divorce hearing was scheduled for a week after her testimony. Juan received a letter from criminal court as well to give testimony. Juan and Melody agreed to ride together.................................

The day of the hearing Melody awakened early. She dressed in a navy blue business dress suit. When Juan came to pick her up he commented on how sexy she looked. Melody felt self conscious because she didn't want to draw any attention.

"Should I change?"

Juan looked at her confused.

"Why would you do that?"

"I don't want anyone looking at me that way."

"Woman it doesn't matter what you put on, you are a good looking and desirable woman."

They left her apartment and got into his car. Juan noticed that she was nervous. He placed his hand over hers and squeezed it.

When they arrived at the court house Juan dropped Melody off and went to park the car. She waited for him. When he walked up to her they walked into the court house together. Although they did not touch Melody could feel comfort from Juan. They set down next to each other, but made sure they did not touch.

Melody noticed when Bill came into the court room. He surveyed the court room. She watched as he entered. Bill was well dressed, something that she admired that about him. She thought, "He is very handsome. How could he be so cruel? What was it about me that made him so angry?"

Bill looked around and then spotted her. He gave her one of his charming smiles. She looked away. She looked at Juan. Melody could tell that Juan had seen Bill look at her. Juan had a serious expression on his face. Melody looked forward.

A half hour went by and then the judge came into the court room. They were told to stand up. Just then Melody glanced over at Bill and noticed him looking at her. This time although no words came out he formed the sentence, "How are you?" He seemed like the man she once fell in love with. She turned away.

Once the judge had taken the bench everyone was instructed to sit. Melody looked at Juan, wondering if he had witnessed the event. The expression on his face gave Melody her answer. Juan seemed irritated. She wasn't sure if his irritation was with Bill or with her for looking at him.

While the attorneys made their opening remarks Melody stayed focus on them. The police were called first. After they had been cross examined by Bill's attorney they were released and then Melody was called to the stand.

Melody was asked her name and marital status. Melody looked at Juan and answered separated. Melody focused on the prosecutor, as he asked her questions. When the prosecutor asked her to point Bill out she looked toward Juan for support and then pointed with a shaky hand to Bill. Although it was a brief look, Melody noticed that

Bill was composed. Melody was surprised that when she looked at him he did not appear angry.

When the prosecutor had finished his questioning he turned it over to Bill's attorney. Melody held her hands on her lap and tried not to appear nervous. Melody did not know what she would be asked. The defense attorney began: "Please state your name again please."

"Melody Turner."

"Can you tell me who this gentleman is?" He pointed to Bill.

"He is my husband."

"How long have you been married?"

"Three and a half years."

"Have you ever been separated?"

The prosecutor yelled, "Objection."

The defense attorney said, "Your honor if you would I promise it has a purpose for my question."

"Over ruled. Please answer the question Mrs. Turner."

"No."

"You have never left him?"

"No."

"On the said date when you came home were you alone?"

Melody thought for a second.

"Yes."

"Mrs. Turner you are under oath."

"I was alone."

"Mrs. Turner isn't it true that you are having an affair with Mr. Juan Mattos seated in this court house?"

The prosecutor yelled objection.

"And isn't it true that your husband found out and caught you with this man on the said date?"

"Objection."

Melody's eyes filled up with tears. She sat there staring at Juan. The judge bang his gavel and then called the attorneys to the bench.

The judge asked the defense attorney "What does this have to do with the case?"

"Your honor I'm trying to establish that Mr. Turner was the victim here."

Prosecutor, "Are you kidding me?"

Defense attorney, "How do you know that they didn't jump on him and he wasn't protecting himself?"

The judge thought about it, "I will allow it. You're walking on thin ground. Be careful."

"Mrs. Turner what is your relationship with Mr. Mattos?"

Melody looked at Juan through glassy eyes.

"We're friends."

"Is that what you call it now?"

"Counselor one more remark like that I will remove you from my courtroom."

"Mrs. Turner how long have you been friends with Mr. Mattos?"

"We work at the same place. We talk often."

"Does he ever visit your home?"

"He only came that one time when Bill was choking me. He saved me. He knew something was wrong."

"He sensed it?"

"Yes."

"How did Mr. Mattos come to rescue you at your home?"

"He gave me a ride that day."

"Does he often give you rides home?"

"No. This was the first time."

"Did your husband know about this friend?"

"No. I never brought people around."

"Why not?"

Melody looked at Bill, "I never knew what mood he would be in. You see my husband was abusive. I didn't want anyone to know how he talked or treated me sometimes."

"How did he treat you?"

"He was verbally and physically abusive."

"Did you ever file a restraining order?"

"No."

"Why not?"

"I didn't want anyone to know."

"So you never told anyone?"

"No."

"So why would Mr. Mattos feel that something was wrong?"

"He saw the busies that day and was concerned. I had a black eye and tried to cover it. He gave me a ride home because the bus hadn't come yet."

"Didn't you have a car?"

"Yes, but Bill used it."

"No further questions."

The prosecutor asked to redirect.

"Melody please tell this court your life with Mr. Turner."

Melody looked directly at Bill as she answered, "For most of my life with Bill, he has been controlling. We got married as soon as I finished college. He wanted us to get married before that because he wanted me to remain a virgin. He told me what to wear, what size I should be and (she stood up) he told me that I was fat. I weigh one hundred pounds. I watched what I eat and was always afraid to eat in front of Mr. Turner because he would make comments about me being fat. (Tears clouded her eyes.) There was nothing that I did that made you happy. I loved you. You took me from a loving family and treated me like I was the worst person on earth. You alienated me from my family and I have to admit I let you. I wanted to be the wife that you needed and wanted, but I could never be that could I? You know why because you're so messed up inside that you don't know how to be happy or what would make you happy."

"Mrs. Turner what happened on the day Mr. Turner was arrested?"

"I went to work that day even though I didn't want to because the night before Mr. Turner beat me up. I tried to cover it up because

I didn't want anyone to see it. They always did. When Mr. Mattos saw me that day he asked me about the bruise. He asked me was I alright. I told him that I was fine. After work I was waiting at the bus stop like I always did, when Mr. Mattos offered me a ride. Nothing more. I was hesitant because I was afraid of Bill somehow finding out, but I was tired from the night before so I accepted the ride. I have a car, but Mr. Turner insisted on me taking the bus and he use my car because he didn't want to get dents in his Lexus. When we got close to where I reside I had Mr. Mattos drop me off a block away from my house because I didn't want any problems. When I entered my house Mr. Turner grabbed me from behind and began choking me. I don't remember anything else until I woke up in the hospital."

"Prior to that day, had you ever gone out or given your husband any reason to be jealous?"

"No. In my entire life I have never looked at anyone lustful or thought of being with anyone else."

"Thank you Mrs. Turner. No further questions."

The judge excused her. Melody walked back to where she was seated. When she sat down Melody wanted to go into Juan's arms and he wanted to comfort her, but they both resisted the temptation. She sat as close as she dare. He comforted her just by his close proximity. Juan was called to the stand. He was sworn in. The prosecutor asked him to state his full name.

"Mr. Juan Mattos."

"Mr. Mattos what is your relationship with Mrs. Turner?"

Juan looked directly into Bills eyes.

"Mrs. Turner and I are friends."

"Have you ever witness any of the abuse that Mrs. Turner spoke of today?"

"Prior to that day I had never actually witnessed the abuse first hand until that day when I stopped Mr. Turner from choking Mrs. Turner. I have seen the busies on Mrs. Turner on several occasions."

"No further questions."

The judge said, "Cross examine."

Defense, "No questions."

The judge adjourned the case and scheduled Bill to return for a verdict.

After they left the courtroom Bill walked over to Melody.

"You look gorgeous today. Can I talk to you?"

"No."

"Come on we can make this work."

"Bill its over." Bill grabbed Melody's arm.

Juan put his hand over Bill's. "Man you want to remove your hand?"

"This is my wife."

"The lady told you she don't want to speak to you."

"Man this don't concern you."

"I'm only going to say this one more time. Let the lady go."

Bill let go of Melody's arm. She and Juan walked off. They walked out of the court house. Melody walked with Juan to get the car because she was afraid that Bill would bother her if she stayed alone. When they got to the car Juan opened the door for her. Melody looked into his eyes and he could tell that she wanted to be held, but to keep up appearances she held back. She got into the car. Juan then got into the car and pulled off. Melody was shaking.

"Are you alright?"

"I don't know. I feel sick."

"My house is closer."

Juan drove to his house. He parked the car and then got out. He walked over to the passenger side and opened the door. He helped Melody out of the car.

"I'm sick."

Melody put her hand up to her mouth. Juan put his arm around her and helped her into the house. Once in the house Melody ran to the bathroom. Juan stood at the bathroom door.

When she came out Juan asked, "Are you alright?"

"Juan I don't know how to tell you this."

Juan's expression changed. He was afraid that Melody had decided to go back to Bill. He was quiet a few minutes.

"What is it?"

"I'm pregnant."

He looked at her.

"What are you going to do?"

"I don't understand."

"Are you going to let Bill know?"

Melody looked confused. Then it dawned on her.

"Juan it's your baby."

He looked at her, as if he was waiting to hear her say that it was a joke. Melody waited patiently until it sank in.

"I don't understand."

"What don't you understand? I haven't been with anyone other than you. I went to the doctor. I'm three months. (Juan was still in shock) Melody smiled at him and gave him a reassuring look. "Bill always used condoms. Besides that we hadn't done anything in months. Remember he was in jail. Remember that night and then that day? You don't have to worry about it. I'll take care of it by myself. You know I had wanted to have a baby for some time and Bill didn't want one. Bill said that he wasn't ready for all that. I already love this baby. I won't mention that I'm pregnant at my divorce because I don't want them to think that it's Bill and I don't want him bothering me. I just want to be free of him and go on with my life. We didn't make a mistake. I wasn't thinking that night nor shall I say not that anyway."

"Do you love me?"

Melody looked into Juan's eyes. He looked desperate. "Yes."

He took Melody's hands and got on one knee. Melody looked down at him.

"Will you marry me?"

They both laughed thinking of their situation.

"Yes I will."

Juan took her into his arms and kissed her.

"I can't believe this. I'm going to be a daddy." He rubbed Melody's stomach. "Come over here and sit down." Melody sat on his lap. "Melody."

"Yes."

"Stay here."

"I didn't bring any clothes to stay the night."

"No, I don't mean just tonight. Live here with me."

Melody looked at him and considered the question. "I guess I could."

"It won't be long before we get married. As soon as your divorce is final I want us to get married. I want our child to have my name through marriage. Is that alright with you? It's not too soon is it?"

"What's too soon. My life is what it is. I love you and I want what you want."

The next week Melody went for her divorce hearing. Juan went with her. Melody was given half of everything Bill had. He was also ordered to pay her half of what the house was worth. The judge granted her the divorce. Bill said nothing. Throughout the hearing Bill was stone faced.

When Juan and Melody left the court house they returned to his home. They ordered in. Melody felt relieved and it showed. Juan was surprised when Melody set a date for their marriage. They scheduled a small ceremony a week after Melody's divorce was finalized. Melody invited a few family members. She was happy to see her parents. They were equally excited and happy that she was no longer married to Bill……………………..

During the ceremony her mother cried and father got teary eyed. Melody eyes were filled with tears for she was very happy.

After the ceremony Juan was welcomed into their family. The couple had the reception in their backyard. Everyone at the wedding seemed to not only be celebrating the wedding ceremony, but for the guest that knew Melody, they celebrated her freedom from Bill.

At midnight everyone began leaving.

After their guest were gone Melody and Juan laid down for a few minutes.................

The two soon got up to leave for the airport. They had a flight to leave for their honeymoon.

When they arrived at the airport the couple had to rush because their plane was boarding. Once they boarded the plane and were seated Melody laid her head on Juan's shoulder and they fell asleep. They slept throughout the ride....................

The couple awakened when they arrived in the Bahamas. They left the plane and got their luggage.

When they stepped outside of the airport there was a car waiting to take them to their hotel.

When they arrived at the hotel the couple checked in. They went up to their room. Juan picked Melody up and carried her into the suite. He carried her over to the bed. Juan sat on the bed, still holding Melody he kissed her. Melody wrapped her arms around Juan's neck.

"I love you so much."

"And I you." Juan put his hand on her stomach. "And you too little one."

Juan layed back still holding onto Melody. He smoothed his hand over her face. They began to kiss. Juan made love to his new bride as if it was the first time. Melody watched her husband as he made love to her. She had never felt the desire that he made her feel that night. Melody could not remember ever being looked at the way that Juan was looking at her now. She thought to herself, "This man really loves me." She then kissed her new husband passionately and made him feel pleasure that he had never felt with any other. The couple made love throughout the day..............................

Later that night they ordered in. Juan and Melody fed each other and talked of their future. After Melody had fallen asleep Juan watched her slow even breathes. Juan couldn't believe that not more than seven months earlier he had desired this woman, not really believing that one day she would be his. He kissed her lightly on the lips and then thanked God for his blessing. Juan soon drifted off to sleep.

During their honeymoon the couple toured the island and often went out on the beach...............................

Their last day on the island the couple stayed in. They ate in their room and lounged on the balcony. Juan held Melody and they both felt secure in their love for each other........

When they awakened the next morning the couple hated to leave. They gathered their things together and then left the room. When they entered the lobby their ride was waiting. Melody stayed close to Juan throughout the ride to the airport.

Once on the plan Melody snuggled close to Juan and soon drifted off to sleep. Juan held her securely and leaned his head on hers. He kissed Melody on the top of her head. He too drifted off to sleep.

When Melody and Juan got back from their honeymoon there was a message on the telephone voicemail that Bill was sentenced to five years in prison and five years probation. Melody thought what the letter meant was that she could now breathe.

Chapter 6

The couple began thinking of their future. They talked of converting one of the guest rooms to a baby room.

As the days passed Melody and Juan were inseparable at home and at work. Melody actually enjoyed work more, now that no one gossiped about her bruises and because of their respect for Juan she was treated better. At night she after she and Juan had made love, before falling asleep Melody thanked God and prayed if this was a dream not to wake her. Every morning she looked over. Once seeing Juan she smiled and thanked God for keeping her dreaming. Melody would kiss Juan and often be lost in his desire.

Melody's pregnancy was going along They visited Melody parent's home on holidays. They wrote and sent pictures to Juan's parents in Puerto Rico. Melody and Juan took some of the money that she received in her divorce and added onto Juan's home.

When she had the baby Melody took leave from work. They had a girl. The baby was named Juanita Margox Mattos.

Juan's parents came to visit their granddaughter a week after the baby was born. Melody's mother left when Juan's parents arrived. Melody was happy that she and her parents were closer than they had ever been. They loved Juan and treated him like the son they never had. Juan's parents didn't speak English well, but they were able to communicate through Juan and his parents spoke broken English. Juan had also taught Melody some Spanish. His parents adored their granddaughter.

When it was time for them to leave they asked if Juan would come visit them when the baby gets older. The couple said that they would.

Juan and Melody decided that she would stay home to raise their daughter. Melody enjoyed being home with Juanita. Melody couldn't believe how happy she was. Juan was very gentle, attentive, caring and took good care of his wife and daughter. Melody saw her parents often and she was happy for that……………………………..

When Juanita turned one year old they threw her a birthday party. Juan's parents came back to visit and stayed two weeks. Melody's parents came and a few people from work were invited. Juan and Melody talked of having another child, but decided they would wait.

For their second anniversary the couple decided to visit Juan's parents for two weeks. Melody enjoyed the country side. She took lots of pictures and decided to make a photo album or more of a memory book for Juanita. Melody learned Spanish well and Juan taught Juanita. She wanted her daughter to learn and know both of the cultures she was from. Melody made a family tree where both families were traced as far back as she could find. She continued to search for more information...................

When they returned from Puerto Rico Melody thought about her in-laws, while they were nice enough Juan's parents didn't seem warm when it came to her. She often wondered if they thought that she was damaged or tainted because of her previous marriage. Melody never let on about her suspicion and took comfort that Juan's parents seemed to love Juanita.

Soon after returning home Melody decided to go back to school. She chose to go into psychology. Melody already had an associates. Juanita was placed in nursery school. Melody went to school during those hours.

Melody received her bachelor's degree in less than three years. Juan was very supportive and proud of his wife. Melody went on to get her graduates degree and Juanita began kindergarten.

A year and a half later Melody received her Graduates degree. Melody and Juan threw a party. They set up the backyard and invited all of their family and friends. Everyone marveled at how smart Juanita was. She was now going to first grade, but was articulate and very advanced for her five years. When people asked Juanita how she get so smart she would tell them that she goes to college with her mommy.

One of Melody's friends informed her that Bill was getting out on Parole in a month. Melody tried not to let it bother, or worry her. She and Juan talked about it and he assured her that everything would be fine. Melody went on to get her doctorates. Medical school was a little more difficult, so Juan took over some of the duties around the house.

Melody made sure that weekends were spent with the family. The family would go to the movies and occasionally out to dinner. They had movie night once a week, where one of them would pick out a family movie.

Once a month Melody's parents would keep Juanita for the weekend so Melody and Juan could spend time with each other one on one. Many times the couple would stay in and transform the den into an exotic place or just simply watch an R rated movie...........

Monday morning Melody had an early morning with one of her courses. She got Juanita up and dressed her.

While she was driving Juanita to school Melody heard a car horn. She glanced to her right. She took a quick look, but did not recognize the person. She continued driving. A block away she stopped at a red light. The person blew their horn again. She had more time to look this time. When she looked over her heart began racing. It was Bill. He had grown a mustache and goatee. He smiled at her. She did not smile back. He spoke through closed windows. Melody cautiously nodded her head. When the light turned she pulled off. Although it was not time for her to turn, Melody made a left at the next corner. She glanced back to see if Bill had followed her. She did not see him turn after her. Melody turned a few more times, taking a different way to Juanita's school.

When she arrived at Juanita's school Melody was shaking.

"What wrong mommy?"

"Nothing baby."

"You're shaking."

"I'm ok." Melody didn't know what to tell her daughter. She didn't want to alarm her.

After dropping Juanita at the school Melody surveyed the street after coming out of the school. She drove to the college with no incident.

When she arrived back at home Melody had a hard time concentrating on her assignment. Melody tried to pull herself together. When she could not pull it together Melody called Juan. He tried to comfort her as much as he could on the phone. He told her that he would pick Juanita up.

When he came home Juan took Melody into his arms and held her. Juanita knew something was going on, so she went up to the couple and put her arms around them. Juan picked her up. He tickled her.

That night they all helped in cooking dinner. The family sat and ate. Although Melody tried to act as if nothing was going on she was quiet and Juanita noticed. Juanita got out of her chair and hugged her mother. Melody returned her affection.

After dinner the family sat together and read stories. An hour later it was time for Juanita to go to bed.

After putting Juanita to bed Juan and Melody sat in front of the fireplace. She laid in Juan's arms. They sat for a while basking in the tranquility of watching and listing to the crackling of the fire. Juan saw Melody dozing off. He lifted her into his arms and carried her upstairs.

The next morning Juan awakened. He got Juanita up and helped her get ready for school. He kissed Melody. Juanita walked over to her bed and kissed her mother. Melody told them bye and they left. Melody went back to sleep.

When she awakened Melody got up and dressed for school. She got into her car. Just as she was placing her seat belt on her cell phone went off. She answered it.

"Hi Mrs. Mattos?"

"Yes."

"This is St. Barnabas Medical Center. We have your husband and daughter here."

"Who is this? Where are you calling from?"

"This is Dr. Lea at St. Barnabas Medical Center. Your husband and daughter were in a bad car accident."

Melody's heart dropped.

"No, they left for work. He took her to school."

"Mrs. Mattos you need to get to the hospital."

Melody hung up the phone. She began driving. Melody began to cry. Through tear filled eyes she strained her eyes to see............................

Forty-five minutes later she arrived at the hospital. Melody parked her car and then ran into the hospital. Melody walked up to the information desk. She gave her name. The receptionist directed her to where Juan and Juanita were. She looked at her baby, hooked up to tubes and machines. She touched her hand and talked to her daughter. Tears ran down her face. She then went into the next room where Juan was also hooked up to machines. Melody laid her head on his chest, lightly, not to hurt him. His breathing was unsteady.

"Juan don't leave me. You have to get better."

Juan struggled to put his arm around Melody.

"Melody" Juan whispered. Melody looked up at him. He struggled to open his eyes. "I love you. Don't quit. You're strong."

"What are you saying? Juan I love you too. Stay with me. I can't live without you."

"Yes you can. You're strong."

Melody felt the life go out of his body.

"Juan. Please, don't leave me. Juan!" Tears streamed her face. The crash team ran into the room. She was asked to leave the room. They worked on Juan a few minutes and then it was over. The doctor came out and put his hand on Melody's arm. Melody ran to her daughter. She took Juanita's small hand.

"Mommy."

"Hi baby. Mommy's here."

"Mommy daddy's here."

"I know baby."

"He wants me to come with him."

"Baby stay with me."

"Mommy, daddy said he loves you. I love you too mommy."

"I love you and daddy."

Melody felt something near her and then it was gone. The crash team ran into the room.

Melody said in a low tone, "Let her go. She's with her father now."

The doctor said, "Is there anyone we can call?"

Melody sat with a tear drenched face not knowing what to do.

"Maim can we call someone?"

Melody continued to sit there and then in a defeated voice she said, "My parents."

Melody pulled out her cell phone. With shaky hands Melody opened it and as if in slow motion pushed the numbers. The phone began to ring. Melody heard her mother pick up the phone and said hello. She handed the phone to the nurse.

"Hello."

"Hello. Melody?"

"No maim. This is the social services department at St. Barnabas. We have your daughter here."

"What's wrong? Is she ill?"

"No maim. She needs someone to be with her right now."

"Tell her me and her father are on our way."

Melody's mother hung up the phone and then went into the den.

"Honey, something's happened. The hospital just called and said that we need to get there. Something about Melody needing someone to come there."

"What else did they say?"

"Nothing."

Her father got up and they left. He drove to the hospital. He dropped her mother off in front of the emergency room and then went to park the car. After Mr. Thomas parked the car he headed to the emergency entrance. He and Mrs. Thomas walked in together. They were directed into the social service area. When they walked in the couple saw Melody sitting alone with her head in her lap. Both parents walked over to Melody.

Mrs. Thomas asked "Baby what's wrong?"

At first Melody was non-responsive. Finally Melody looked up with a tear drenched face. She looked almost in a trance.

"They're gone."

Her mother asked, "Who's gone?"

"The love of my life."

"What happened to Juan?"

"He and Juanita was…" Melody couldn't speak the words.

Mr. Thomas left the room. He went to talk with the social worker. When Mr. Thomas returned he had tears in his eyes. He took Melody into his arms. Mrs. Thomas looked at him. He whispered, "Juan and Juanita were in a car accident. They didn't' make it." His voice cracked. The three sat in the quiet cold room, not speaking, not able to formulate any words. They sat there for an hour trying to collect themselves. The social worker came into the room and asked if there was anything she could do. Melody was asked to sign forms. Mechanically she signed the forms and still in her father's arms allowed him to lead her to their car. Mr. Thomas helped Melody into the car.

He then turned to Mrs. Thomas.

"Can you drive?" Mrs. Thomas shook her head yes. "Okay, I'll get Melody's car and I'll meet you at home."

Melody said, "I want to go home."

Mrs. Thomas commented, "We are baby."

She looked at her mother, "My home."

Mrs. Thomas looked at Mr. Thomas. He nodded his head in agreement with Melody. He kissed his daughter on the forehead. Mrs. Thomas got into the car. Mr. Thomas closed the door behind her. He got Melody's keys and left. Mr. Thomas walked to Melody's car. He got in and started it. The radio was on. The news man reported, "Special report. There was a fatal accident on Route 22, West Bound. Tune into channel nine news at six for more information. Mr. Thomas searched the stations for more details. He thought to himself, "It can't be the same accident." He decided to detour. Mr. Thomas drove as close as he could before he had to detour. He thought, "That looks like Bill's car." He drove to Melody's home. When he got to her house he checked to see how Melody was doing. She had gone into her bedroom and laid down. He kissed her on the forehead.

"Hi sweetheart." Melody looked up. Her eyes were red from crying. She had a far away look. Melody did not speak. Her father sat on the bed beside her and put his hand on her shoulder. "Daddy's here." He sat a few minutes and then said, "I'm going downstairs with your mother. We'll be right downstairs."

When he went downstairs Mrs. Thomas was sitting in the den. Although the television was on she was not watching it. Her eyes were glassy and she seemed to be in a daze. When she heard her husband Mrs. Thomas looked up at him.

"I can't believe it."

"Me either."

Tears formed in her eyes. Mr. Thomas walked over to her and sat next to her. He put his arms around her. She laid her head on his chest.

"Charles what are we going to do?"

"We have to be strong for Melody."

"I don't understand what happened."

"Wait. Turn that up." He pointed to the television. Mrs. Thomas turned the television up.

"There was a two car crash this morning. It appears that one car sped up and crashed into the other. This man witnessed this fatal crash." (They showed the medic, police and firemen at the scene.) "Yes I was driving on the right side of 22 and I saw this Lexus speed up to this 357. The man pulled along the side of the car and looked like he was trying to run him off the road. The 357 tried to speed up and then I saw the little one in the back seat. I couldn't believe when the Lexus started chasing the 357 and caught up with it, with that baby in the back. Oh my goodness! He rammed them. The car swirl, but he gained control. The Lexus hit him again. This time harder and the 357 hit the guard rail, spin around, hit the Lexus, it went into the lake and the other car into the concrete wall. Pieces flew, other cars swerved to avoid hitting the car and tried to get out of the way. I couldn't believe it. When they pulled that baby out I prayed. That man was all cut up. I don't know what happened to the guy in the Lexus. I don't think he made it. I hope those other two made it."

"Thank you Dr. Davis."

"Tell those people our prayers are with them."

"I think that other car was Bill."

"Do you really think so?"

"Yes."

"Why did he do this? It's been five years."

"He couldn't be happy and he didn't want Melody to be happy either. I guess he couldn't let go."

"I'm going up to check on Melody."

Mrs. Thomas went up to Melody's bedroom. When she entered the room Melody was asleep.

Melody called out, "Juan."

Mrs. Thomas' heart broke.

"Baby it's mom."

"Mom."

"Yes baby."

"Mom what am I going to do? My family's gone."

Mrs. Thomas went over to Melody and hugged her. She held her for a while. Mr. Thomas came up with soup for three. While Melody only had a few spoonfuls, her parents were happy for that. Melody's parents tried to make light conversation. Her parents stayed with her until she fell asleep.

Once Melody was asleep they went to one of the guest rooms. On their way to the room they stopped at Juanita's room. They looked in. Their eyes filled up with tears seeing pictures of the child and all of the things that made Juanita who she was.

The next day the hospital called. Mrs. Thomas answered the phone. After speaking with them Mrs. Thomas went up to discuss the matter with Melody. Melody asked her mother to call her mother-in-law.

Three days later funeral arrangements were made.

A day before the funeral Melody received a call from the coroner about Bill. She was still named as his next of kin. She told them to cremate him. She remembered him always saying that was what he wanted. Juan's parents flew in. They stayed at a hotel. They couldn't bring themselves to go to the house. Melody held everything at the church.

After the repast Melody returned home alone. She assured her parents that she needed to be home alone. She thanked them for being there for her.

When Melody opened her front door she felt a presence there. As Melody walked up the stairs she envisioned Juanita going into her room. Melody went into her daughter's room. She sat on the bed. Everything had been left the way Juanita left it. On the bed was a small photo album. Melody looked in it. It had pictures of their family. Melody ran her hand over the pictures, remembering how happy they were. Melody layed down. She hugged Juanita's favorite stuff animal. Tears streamed her eyes. After a while Melody fell asleep.

She began to dream:

Melody was in her home sitting on the couch. Juan came home. Melody said, "Where have you been?"

"I went to pick up Juanita."

Juanita came running into the room.

"Hi baby."

Juanita ran over to Melody and hugged her.

"I miss you mommy."

"I miss you too baby."

Juan took Juanita upstairs. Melody started up behind them. As the three climbed the staircase Juan and Juanita began to fade. Melody called out to them, but they were gone.

Melody began to cry in her sleep. She woke herself up. The pillow that she had been laying on was wet. Melody got out of bed and went into her bedroom. Melody went into the bathroom and turned on the shower. She removed her clothes and got in. Melody stood under the water and cried. She washed her face. As Melody began to wash her body she remembered showering with Juan. She longed for his touch. Melody cried out, "God" asking God to give her strength. She eventually turned the shower off, but did not step out. Melody sat on the floor of the shower and continued to cry. She remained there and drifted off to asleep.

When morning came Melody was still asleep. The ringing of the telephone awakened her. She looked around and realized where she was. Melody stood up and wrapped a towel around herself. Melody slowly walked to the phone. It was her in-laws. They told her that they were returning home and that they wished her well. Melody told them that she was sorry for their lost. Melody thought to herself, "If Juan had never married me, he would still be alive. If my baby had not been mine she would not have died. Bill finally succeeded in taking everything from me." As if talking to Bill she asked, "Why did you hate me so much? What did I do so wrong?" She yelled "God help me? I can't do this by myself." She lowered her voice, "Take care of my husband and baby. Tell them that I love them."

Melody began to clean her house. She tried to keep busy.

Chapter 7

The next week Melody tried to return to school. She tried to throw herself into her school work. Melody was thankful for the distraction.

A month went pass. Although it was difficult Melody continued her studies. Melody had promised Juan that she would. One of the Doctors, Collin Miller took her under his wing.

Melody was happy that there was someone that she could talk to, someone other than her family. She knew that they meant well, but she felt they pitied her. Collin didn't know her background or what happened just a few months before meeting him.

Melody remembered when she first met Collin. She was sitting in the student lounge trying to study, but couldn't concentrate. Collin had noticed her and walked over. He introduced himself and asked if

90

she was alright. At first Melody just stared at him. It was only after Collin repeated his question that Melody answered, "No."

Collin asked if he could sit with her. After that it was as if Collin and Melody became friends. Melody would sometimes go to his office after class just to talk, not of anything important. There were also times when she came to his office for a word of encouragement. He never disappointed her. Melody was always careful not to talk about her personal life. She didn't want to be pitied.

As the months went by Melody began getting rid of Juan and Juanita's things. She donated them to the shelter.

One day after coming from school Melody took the mail out of the box. She sorted through it. There was one letter that caught her attention. It was from a lawyer's office. Melody opened it. Melody read the letter. She didn't understand what it meant. Melody called the attorney. The attorney answered.

"Hi, My name is Melody Mattos. I received a letter from your office regarding Bill Turner. I don't understand why I received it."

"Oh, yes, Mrs. Mattos, you are the beneficiary of Mr. Turner's estate."

"I don't' understand."

"Mr. Turner left all of his belongings to you. I need you to come in and sign for them at your earliest connivance." Melody was dumb founded. "Mrs. Mattos, are you there?"

"Yes. I don't understand."

"I have a Will here and it names you as the sole inheritor. When can you come down to my office and take care of this matter? I have been trying to reach you for some time now."

"I guess I can come after class tomorrow."

"What time will that be?"

"Three o'clock. Is that ok?"

"Yes. That's fine."

"Ok, then I'll see you tomorrow at 3."

"I look forward to meeting you."

When Melody went to bed she thought about the phone call and was bewildered. She laid awake most of the night questioning why Bill had not changed his Will. Then she thought to herself, "I guess there wasn't anyone else to leave it to." After tossing and turning Melody finally drifted off to sleep.

The next morning Melody awakened early. She got dressed and left for school. Melody happened to run into Collin. He walked up to Melody and hugged her. He kissed her on the forehead.

"Hey. How are you?"

"I'm doing okay."

"Are you? You know you can always come to me for anything."

"Can I talk to you in your office?"

"Sure. Come on." He put his hand on the lower part of her back to direct her to his office. Dr. Miller opened his door and Melody walked in. "So what can I help you with?"

"I received a letter yesterday from my ex-husband's attorney. Apparently he left everything in my name. I have to go there after I'm finish here today."

"Really? How do you feel about that?"

"Uneasy. I don't understand if he hated me so much, why would he leave everything to me?"

"Maybe it was an over site."

'He wasn't like that."

"Why do you think he hated you?"

"He abused me. He took my family from me. What else would you call it?"

"I think in his own mind he believed your family took you from him. His controlling was his way of keeping you where he needed you to be for him."

"I still don't understand it."

"You may not understand, but that is what he believed."

"If you say so. Well I better go."

"Look if you ever need me, here is my cell phone number." (He handed Melody his business card) "My personal number is on the back." (He turned it over) "You can call me anytime."

"Thank you so much." Melody took the card. She put it in her pocket. She was able to get through the rest of her classes.

When it was time to leave school Melody felt sick. She sat in her car and prayed for God to help her to be calm. After sitting there twenty minutes Melody turned on her car. As she went to pull off

Melody heard a car horn. She looked. It was Collin. She pulled back into the parking space and beeped the horn. She got out of her car. He pulled up and rolled his window down. Melody walked up to his window.

"What's up?"

"Can I ask a favor?"

"Sure."

"Is it possible for you to come with me to the attorney's office today?"

"I can do that."

"Are you sure? I'm not taking you from anything am I?"

"No. Get in. I'll drive and then we can come back and get your car."

"Are you sure? I don't want to inconvenience you."

"Don't worry about it. I'm happy to be of assistance."

Melody gave Collin the address. As they drove to the attorney's office Melody was quiet. Collin sensed her nervousness and made light conversation. After a while without understanding why Melody opened up to Collin. She told him of her life with Bill. He quietly listened, not making any comments.

When they arrive at the office Collin parked. He and Melody got out of the car. They went into the attorney's office. Melody gave her name to the receptionist. After a few minutes the attorney came out. He held his hand out. Melody shook it.

"Hi, I'm Mr. Davis, your ex-husband's attorney."

"Hi Mr. Davis, this is Dr. Miller."

Mr. Davis extended his hand.

"How do you do?"

"Fine. Thank you."

"Follow me."

Melody and Collin followed Mr. Davis.

When they entered the room Mr. Davis said, "Have a seat. Ms. Mattos."

"Mrs. Mattos."

"Excuse me. Mrs. Mattos you have inherited the estate of a Mr. Turner. This estate consist of his home, pension two hundred thousand dollars, life insurance a million dollars, his car insurance doubled indemnity five hundred thousand dollars, he had some other assets such as savings, bonds and mutual funds which total another million dollars. I need you to sign this and then I can release everything to you."

"I still don't understand."

"He had you down as the next of kin on his paperwork and you are the beneficiary on all of his policies."

"But we were divorced."

"I understand that. We spoke about that. He said that no one was as deserving or worthy of his belongings." Melody looked at the attorney in disbelief. "He really loved you."

"He had a horrible way of showing it."

"I know." Melody looked at him curiously. "He was also my friend. He talked to me about you. Bill used to say that he knew he hurt you, but he couldn't help himself. He said that he was always afraid that you would leave him. He didn't understand why you stayed. He knew you loved him. When you finally left him he said that although he was relieved, because he hated hurting you, his life was over. When he went to prison he told me to put everything in your name in case of his death. He didn't want you to have to pay an inheritance tax or have any problems obtaining these gifts. It was his way of asking for your forgiveness."

Mr. Davis showed Melody where to sign the papers. When she was finished signing the papers Mr. Davis said, If you need any help with anything feel free to contact me." He gave Melody his card. He took her hand in his. "If you need anything, anything at all." He looked at her not as an attorney. It was something else in his eyes that caused her to looked at him curiously.

Collin was looking on.

Collin interrupted by asking, "Is that it?"

Mr. Davis looked at Collin and smiled. Collin knew that look and gave Mr. Davis an disapproving looked.

"Yes that's it." Davis stood up. "It has been a pleasure to meet you." He took Melody's hands. "You know he was right about you."

"What was that?"

"You're beautiful and make a guy want to take care of you. Remember anything at all."

"Thank you Mr. Davis."

"Larry please."

Collin said, "Well Mr. Davis it has been interesting. I think I should take Mrs. Mattos home now. This is a lot for her to take in. Thank you for your assistance."

The men shook hands. They looked at each other as if in a competition. After a few minutes of the men flexing they simultaneously released each other's hands. Melody stood up. Collin put his hand on the lower part of Melody's back. He looked at her.

"Are you ready?"

"Yes."

Mr. Davis said, "I'll call you when all of the checks are made out."

"That's fine."

When Melody and Collin got into his car he turned it on. He looked at Melody.

"I'm starving. Let's go out to eat. My treat."

"Are you sure? I don't want to take up all of your time."

"Don't worry about it. Enjoy life. You have to learn to relax and experience life."

"I think I've experienced too much of life's disappointments."

"I agree you have experienced the sadder state of life."

Melody looked at him.

"I don't understand."

"Your life with Bill. Then as you say you were ecstatically happy for a short time and your state now. But what you don't understand is there's more. There will be brighter days. Hey Larry seemed to be interested in you."

Melody looked at Collin curiously at the way he said Mr. Davis' name.

"He was just being nice."

"Believe me he had an arterial motive."

"Well I can't think of any of that right now. It's a struggle just getting up and then getting through each day."

"It'll get easier."

"What am I going to do with the rest of my life? I never thought that I would end up alone. Honestly I didn't think of my future. With Bill I just lived life day by day praying that I wouldn't hurt any more. When that was over I didn't have time to think of anything because Juan, my second husband was there. He was so strong, I didn't have to be. Come to think of it I didn't take a breath. Things just happened between us and I was in another relationship without really mourning the other." Tears filled up in her eyes and Collin heard her voice crack.

"This is only temporary."

"I don't know. I've been married twice and neither lasted."

"That doesn't mean that if you get into another relationship it won't last."

"I guess that I should be thankful for what I had."

"You can be grateful, but at the same time expect more from your future. We better get going. Where would you like to go?"

"You know I haven't had Mexican in a while. Juan and I use to order from this Mexican restaurant not far from my house."

"Well let's go there."

A half hour later Melody and Collin arrived at the restaurant. Collin parked the car and they walked into the restaurant.

They were seated. Melody and Collin ordered their meal. The server brought them their drinks.

As Melody sipped her drink she smiled.

"You know this is the first drink that I've had in probably three years. On our second anniversary Juan and I came here. My parents watched Juanita. That is my daughter's name. I've forgotten how good these are."

The server brought their food. Melody took a bite of her seafood Fajita. "This is good."

"I guess you haven't had one of these in a long time."

"No I haven't. Would you like to taste it?"

Collin leaned over and bit a piece.

"Hummh, that is good."

Melody sat back in her chair. Collin noticed that she seemed more relaxed.

"It feels nice being here tonight. I'm glad you came with me today."

"Me too."

Melody and Collin was quiet for the rest of their meal. When they were finished their meal the server asked would that be it. Melody said that she couldn't eat another bite. She smiled. Collin asked her what the smile was about. Melody explained about how she ate when she was married to Bill. She then divulged that Juan always encouraged her to eat but insisted that he loved her no matter what size she was. Collin took in the difference in her move.

After paying for the meal they left. Collin drove Melody to her car. She got out of his car. Before closing the door Melody bent down.

"Collin can I ask another favor?"

"Sure. What is it?"

"Can you follow me home?"

"No problem."

Melody got into her car and started it up. She pulled off. Collin followed her.

When they arrived at Melody's home she parked in the driveway. She got out of the car and waved Collin to park next to her. He pulled up and then turned the car off. Melody walked up to his car. Collin rolled the window down.

"Come inside."

"Are you sure?"

"Collin I don't want to be alone."

Collin rolled the window back up, turned the car off and then got out of the car. Melody took him by the hand. They walked into the house. Melody lead him into the living room.

"Would you like a drink?"

"What do you have?"

"Come and see."

Collin walked over to the bar.

"I'll get ice."

Collin fixed two drinks. When Melody returned with ice she put ice in both of their glasses. Melody picked hers up, sipped it and walked over to the love seat. She sat down and folded her legs on the chair. Collin walked over to the couch. He sat down. Holding his drink Collin looked at Melody.

"What?"

"Nothing. I was just thinking how beautiful you are. One day you are going to be very happy."

"You think?"

"I know."

He took a sip of his drink. They were quite for a while. Melody looked down.

"Collin can you hold me?"

At first Collin looked at Melody curiously. She looked sad. He thought to himself, "How can one deny such beauty?" Collin got up and walked over to the love seat. He sat down. Melody moved towards him. Collin placed his arm around her shoulders. Melody laid her head against his chest. Collin took his free hand and caressed her hair. Tears streamed from Melody's eyes. When she sniffled Collin lifted her face to look at her. His heart went out to her. He tried to wipe the tears away, but they continued to come. He took her head and put it to his chest. Collin held her tight and caressed her back. She wrapped her arms around his waist and began to cry. Collin took his handkerchief out of his pocket and gave it to her. Melody wiped her face and then blew her noise. She laid her head back on his chest and put her arms around his waist again.

"Why did God have to take my family?"

"It was just their time."

"That's hard for me to believe. If it wasn't for Bill."

Collin took Melody by her arms and pulled her away from him.

"It doesn't matter how they died. Some people are only on this earth for a short period of time. They're not meant to be with us forever. That's why you have to enjoy every minute of your life."

"I lived and I enjoyed my family and then they were taken away."

Collin held her as she cried. "I'm sorry. We were having such a good time."

"You have no reason to be sorry."

After a while Melody quieted down. Collin leaned back taking Melody with him. He continued to hold her and caressed her back. After a while Melody drifted off to sleep. Collin thought about his situation. He looked down at Melody. He thought her very beautiful and loved the way she felt in his arms. He too soon drifted off to sleep.

Melody stirred and Collin held her tighter.

Melody began to dream. *She was home. Juan and Juanita came into the front door. They walked over to her and kissed Melody. "Where have you been?"*

"I was with daddy."

"Juan where were you?"

"We had to go away. Melody you have to let us go."

"I can't."

"You must. You should be happy. We'll always love you."

"Juan why couldn't you stay?"

"It was my time. I couldn't stay. You must let me go. You are promised happiness and he will stay with you. You will have more babies and you will be loved."

"Juan I want you."

Juan kissed her on the forehead. Juanita hugged Melody. She took Juan's hand.

"Darling I won't be coming back. This is the only way you are going to move on."

"Don't leave me. I'm all alone."

"Darling you're not alone. Open your eyes. Your new life is right in front of you."

Juan and Juanita walked out the door."

Melody woke up and called after her husband and daughter. Collin woke up. He saw Melody sitting up and calling out to Juan. Collin sat up and put his arms around Melody. He pulled Melody to him and held her.

"Melody."

She turned around. With her eyes still closed she kissed Collin. He returned her affection. He wanted to erase her pain. He held her to him and kissed her passionately. Collin laid her back and looked at her. Her eyes were still closed. Collin composed himself.

"Melody."

He smoothed his hand over her face. Melody opened her eyes. She was still glossy eyed. She looked up at Collin.

"Are you alright?"

Melody had not realized what happened.

"I was dreaming about Juan."

"I thought as much."

Melody looked at Collin. She saw something in his expression and then it changed.

"Are you alright? I'm sorry I kept you up all night and I took up your whole day yesterday."

"Don't worry about it. It was a pleasure. I am happy you chose me."

"You are such a good friend."

"Hey are you hungry?"

I could eat something."

"I'll run out, get me a tooth brush and something for us to eat."

"I have some new brushes upstairs in the bathroom and I'll cook something up."

"Are you sure?"

"Yes go up the stairs, it's the second door on the left."

Melody went up to her room and took a quick shower. She put on some lounging clothes. Melody went back downstairs. Collin was sitting on the couch.

"There you are. I went into the kitchen, but you weren't there."

"I went to freshen up. Sorry. I thought I would run up and be back before you were finish."

"That's alright."

"Would you like to keep me company while I cook?"

"Sure."

"What would you like to eat?"

"Surprise me."

Melody prepared a western omelet, Canadian bacon and French toast. She brewed them fresh coffee. When it was done she made two plates and sat them on the table. She put her head down and said a silent prayer. They began to eat.

"Hmmh this is good."

"Thank you."

"I bet your husband enjoyed your meals."

"That's what he used to say, that one of the reasons he married me was because of my cooking."

"I'm sorry. I didn't mean to make you sad."

"You didn't. It's nice talking about him. It's nice being able to cook for someone. It's been some time. I hate eating alone. It's nice having someone to appreciate my cooking."

"Maybe you will invite me over again and fix me dinner."

"I would enjoy that."

They talked well into the afternoon.

"Melody it has been my pleasure spending these two days with you, but I have to get home. I have to work this evening."

"I didn't mean to take up so much of your time. Thank you for being there for me."

Collin stood up. He took Melody's hand. She stood up. They walked to the front door. Collin took both of Melody's hands. He brought them up to his lips. Collin kissed them and then her forehead.

"Call me if you need me. Anytime. Promise?"

"Promise. Bye. Thanks again."

"See you."

Chapter 8

A month later Davis called Melody. He told her that he had her checks ready. He asked her when she would be available to pick them up. Melody told him that she could come by to pick them up now. He said great and they hung up. Melody got dressed and then headed to Davis' office.

A half hour later she arrived at his office. Melody parked her car and then walked into the office. His receptionist had gone home. When Melody walked into the office Davis came out of his office.

"Hi. He walked over as if familiar and kissed her lightly on the cheek. Melody looked at him, surprised at his greeting.

"Come in. Have a seat. I have a few more things for you to sign."

Melody signed several papers. Davis gave her each check separately. Melody looked at each one as Davis handed it to her. She couldn't believe how much she was receiving. After giving her all of the checks, bonds and passbooks, which had been changed into her name, Davis gave her the deed to the house she and Bill had once shared. She looked at it.

"What am I going to do with this?"

"You can sell it."

Melody looked at Davis.

"Are you serious?"

"It's yours. Do you need help with that?"

"I haven't been in that house in over five years."

"Do you need help cleaning it out? I can help."

Melody looked at Davis.

"You would do that for me? Why not?"

Davis took her hands in his.

"I feel like I know you. Bill told me so much about you. I can't believe how he treated you. I would never do anything to hurt you."

Melody looked at him. She couldn't believe what she was hearing, how forward Davis was being. Melody sat quiet for a little while and then she looked at Davis, as if to study who this man was.

"Are you serious?"

"Very."

"I think I'll take you up on that offer."

"Well I was just about to close up. How about dinner?"

Melody looked at Davis curiously. She was taken aback.

"Don't you eat? Besides we can discuss your plans."

"Yes. But."

"But, what? You're not hungry?"

"I hadn't thought about it."

"Well think about it. I would like to take you out to eat. I would like to get to know you first hand. I apologize for me being so forward, but I don't think that I would get too far if I wasn't. Bill told me that you were different from any woman he had ever known. I see what he saw. You are a special woman. I know it hasn't been long since you lost your husband, but I can tell that you have a lot of love to give and I would like to be the lucky guy that you give it to."

All Melody could do is stare at him. She was shock at his conversation and couldn't speak. Davis got up and pulled Melody up by her hands.

"There is a restaurant down the street. We can walk there. The cars will be fine here." Davis continued to hold Melody's hand. Melody didn't try to remove her hand. They walked hand in hand to the restaurant. As they walked Melody thought about what Davis had said.

She didn't know how to react to his statement. "Was it too soon to think about dating? What about the dream? Was this the happiness Juan spoke of? Was this the man that would bring her happiness? What am I doing?"

Davis was so strong willed he left no room for Melody to think. She was ashamed to think that it was actually a turn on. When they made it to the restaurant Davis opened the door. Melody walked in. The host greeted them right away and asked to follow the hostess. As they walked to their table Davis placed his hand behind her back. When they made it over to the table the host held a seat out for

Melody. Melody sat down. They ordered drinks. While they waited for their meal Melody and Davis sipped on their drinks.

When their food was brought to them Davis asked to taste hers. She took his fork off his side of the table. She dipped it in her food. She handed it to him. He ate it seductively. Melody looked away.

"Davis, what you have done for me has been very nice, but I think you have the wrong impression of me."

"I don't think that I do. Everything that Bill told me is true."

"I don't think you should go by everything he told you."

"Everything that he said is true. One thing he said though wasn't actually accurate. You are more beautiful then he described. I've wanted to meet you the very first day he came to my office."

"When did he come to you?"

"Right after he got out of prison."

"What did he say?"

"He told me that he didn't think that he would be living a long time. He wanted to make sure that his ex-wife received all of his belongings."

"Did he say why? Didn't you wonder why?"

"Yes. He said that he was a bad husband and had treated you horribly. He said that he hated how he treated you, but he was so afraid of you leaving him that he did mean things and said things to keep you with him. He said this was his way of making it up to you. I wondered who was this woman that this man couldn't live without, couldn't be happy with or without and wanted to give the world to."

Melody took a bite of her food.

"That is so sexy."

"What?"

"The way that you're eating that?"

"You're making me feel uncomfortable."

"I don't mean to."

"I'm not ready to get into a relationship. You're moving too fast."

"I didn't mean to make you feel uncomfortable. I have been mesmerized by you and meeting you for the first time after hearing so much about you, I just wanted to get to know you. We can take it as slow as you want. I just wanted you know where I stand. By the way what happened to Mr. Miller?"

Melody smiled as she thought about Collin.

"He's a good friend. He is my mentor at school."

"Is that all?"

"Yes. He's never made any advances. He's never expressed any interest."

"Really?"

"Why did you say it like that?"

"I can't imagine any man not wanting to be with you."

"Well he's not."

"You sound disappointed."

"No. He's a nice guy. He's been a good friend."

Davis did not pry any longer, but could not accept her answer. There was something in her voice that told him other wise and something in the way Collin looked at her, him and touched her in their brief meeting that made him think there was something going on between them.

After they finished their meal Davis walked Melody to her car. He stood in close proximity to her.

"So when would you like to meet again to discuss selling your house?" Melody looked confused. "Excuse me. Your ex-husband's house."

"Sorry. So much has happened, in such a short period of time. How about next week?"

"That would be fine. Maybe we can go over the plans over dinner."

"Let me get back to you."

Davis looked into Melody's eyes. She could tell that he wanted to kiss her. He was so close. She could smell his minty breath and the essence of cologne he had sprayed on earlier in the day. Melody smiled and then held her hand out.

"Well Mr. Davis it has been interesting. Thank you so much for all of your help."

He took her hand and brought it up to his lips and kissed it. As he kissed it he looked into Melody's eyes.

"It has been my pleasure. I look forward in meeting with you next week. If you need anything before then, do not hesitate to call me. Remember my private cell is on the reverse side of the card I gave you."

Melody got into her car. She turned it on. Davis moved back. Melody smiled at him and then pulled off. As she drove away, Melody thought about what Davis had told her. She couldn't believe that Bill had said the things that Davis had told her. She couldn't believe that Bill really loved her. Melody was flabbergasted that Davis had come onto her. Her cell phone rang. She answered it.

"Hello."

"Hi."

"Collin?"

"What, you were expecting someone else?"

"No. I was just surprise that you called."

"I know I've been busy. I've been meaning to call you. I called to let you know that I am going to a seminar for a week and I won't be around. You can call me if you need me. When I come back I'll call you."

"When are you leaving?"

"Next Monday."

"Oh."

Collin heard something in her voice, "What's wrong?"

"Nothing."

"Tell me Melody."

"I just left Mr. Davis. (Collin looked at the time) I picked up the checks."

"Oh. Why did he have you there this late?"

"He called me earlier. We went out to eat."

Collin was silent for a few minutes.

"What was that about?"

Melody thought to herself, "Is he jealous or a concerned friend? He's never expressed any interest in me."

"You were right. After I signed the papers he asked me out to eat. He said that he's wanted to meet me ever since Bill told him about me."

"Really?"

"I was surprised as well."

"So are you interested?"

"He asked me to go out to eat again next week, after we discuss selling Bill's house."

"Are you going?"

"I told him that I would think about it. What do you think?"

"You're asking me?"

"You're my friend."

"That's something that you have to decide for yourself."

"Do you think that he's okay?"

"Melody while I'm your friend, I am a man."

Melody thought about the comment.

"I don't understand."

"You can't ask a man about dating another man. I am here for you, but I won't tell you whether to date him or not. My ideas are tainted. Do you think that you're ready to date now?"

"I don't know, but I thought about the other night when you stayed over. I had a dream of Juan that night. He and Juanita. He told me that I had to let him go. He told me happiness is waiting for me and the only way that I will have it is by letting him go."

"So you think this Davis character may be it?"

"I don't know. I just thought that I would talk to him and see how it goes. I told him that I wanted to take it slow."

"So you have thought about taking him up on his offer?"

"Yes I have. Will you stay my friend?"

"Melody I'll always be here for you. All you have to do is call. By the way what is it that you wanted my help in?"

"I have all of this money and from someone who was abusive. I would like to do something good with some of it."

"Maybe we can get together and put our minds together and come up with something. When would you like to get together?"

"How about you come over Sunday? I'll cook you dinner. That's if you are available."

"I'm always available for a home cook meal and you cooking I'll make myself available. I've tasted you, so I know what to expect."

Melody looked at the phone. She thought of his words. Melody wondered if it was a slip of the tongue? She decided that he was talking of the breakfast that she had cooked for him.

"Okay I'll see you then."

"What time?"

"Four. We can have drinks before we eat."

"Sounds like a plan. See you Sunday."

"Okay. Bye."

Melody hung up the phone. She smiled at the thought of Collin being jealous of Davis. She wondered, "Are both of these men attracted to me? Collin hasn't expressed interest, but I wonder. How can I be thinking of these men when the love of my life is gone. Am I wrong for even entertaining the thought of moving on? Will the next man make me feel the way Juan did? Will that person be as generous, loving, or interesting? Can I fall in love with another man? Will I have any more children? Will I be able to have any more children? I miss my family. God give me strength. I need your help. I'm so alone. Tell my darlings that I love them."

Melody entered her house. It was so quiet. She went up to her bedroom. Melody laid in bed. Tears filled her eyes. She began to cry. Melody cried herself to sleep............

The next day she got up, showered and got dressed. She noticed that her clothes were not fitting as well as they had. She had lost weight. She remembered how Juan used to try to get her to eat more. Then Melody thought of how Bill used to tell her that she was too fat. Melody had dropped a size since both of them had died. She looked at herself. "Am I too thin?" Melody left and headed to class. She dropped into Collin's office. He got up and kissed her on the side of her face.

"How are you?"

"I'm doing alright."

"Are you eating?"

"Why?"

"You've lost weight."

"You think?"

"I know. Those pants use to fit your hips."

Melody teased. "You've been looking at my behind?"

"It's hard not to."

Melody looked at him as if she was shocked.

"Was I fat?"

"Let me just tell you not that you don't look good now, but you were filling those pants out."

Melody blushed.

"Do you think that I was fat?"

"Fat? You are perfect. You look good this way and you looked good when you had more meat on your bones. What are you about one hundred and five pounds?"

"Maybe. I was one seventeen."

"And you think that's fat?"

"Bill always said that I was fat and Juan told me what you're telling me now."

"Juan was a smart man."

"Yes he was. He was my rock. He helped me be strong enough to leave Bill and he was patient when I was trying to decide what to do. He was a mess too. He use to say things. He would compliment me and say what he would do if I would let him. But when I told him that I needed to think things over he backed off and we remained friends. I loved him so much."

Collin saw the sadness in Melody's eyes. He walked over and put his arms around her. Melody placed her head in his chest and then wrapped her arms around his waist. He held her close to him. Collin caressed her hair and kissed it. They stayed locked in each other arms for a little while.

"Hey how about going out dancing?"

"Dancing?"

"Yes. You need to have some fun."

Collin twirled her around. "Come on let me take you out tonight."

"Tonight?"

"Yes. Do you have any plans for tonight?"

"No."

"Then let me show you a good time. I'll come by at nine. I know a great club."

"Okay." Melody looked at the time. "I better go. I'll see you tonight."

"Okay."

Melody left. When her classes were over Melody went home. She was excited about going dancing. She enjoyed dancing. Both of her husbands were good dancers. Juan was more romantic. He would sometimes take her hand and they would dance to his humming songs. She looked into her closet. Melody took several dresses out of the closet. She laid them on the bed. Melody tried each dress and put on shoes to match. She finally selected one of the dresses, shoes and jewelry to match. Melody showered and sprayed her favorite perfume on. She looked at herself with an approving eye.

Melody heard the doorbell. She went downstairs to open the door. When she opened the door, Collin looked at her and smiled. He leaned over and kissed her on the cheek.

"You look beautiful."

"Thank you."

"Are you ready?"

"Yes."

Collin held his hand out and Melody took it. They walked to his car. Collin opened the car door. Melody got in. Once Collin got into the car he drove off. Collin and Melody talked as he drove to the club...........

When they arrived at the club Collin parked the car. They exited the car. Collin and Melody walked hand in hand to the club. They entered.

"Would you like to dance or get a drink?"

"Let's dance."

Melody led Collin onto the dance floor. They began to dance...............

After several songs a slow song was played. Collin took Melody into his arms. She did not resist. He held her close. They moved to the music. Melody laid her head on Collin's chest. Melody liked the way that she felt in Collin's arms. He made her feel that way Juan did when he held her. They swayed to the music. The couple were lost in the romance of the song.........

When the song was over Collin was hesitant to release her. A fast song began playing. Collin spin Melody around and brought her back into his arms.

"Would you like to get a drink?"

"Yes."

The couple left the dance floor. They ordered drinks. Collin spotted a seat. They walked over to it and sat down.

"So are you having a good time?"

"Yes. It feels like it's been a long time, a life time."

"This is just the beginning."

"You promise?"

"Yes."

Melody saw something in Collin's eyes, something that told her he meant what he promised. Collin and Melody sipped their drinks.

They sat and watched the couples on the dance floor. The two laughed and talked for a while. When they were finished their drinks Collin stood up. He held his hand out.

"Shall we?"

Melody took his hand. He pulled her up to him. He held her close as they walked onto the dance floor. As they danced Melody and Collin were swept away. She didn't think of her past or of her future. Melody lived in this moment. She touched Collin playfully. She moved seductively to the music and Collin responded. He touched her as if familiar and held her body close to his. At one point they looked into each others eyes. For a second Melody thought she saw something in his eyes. She didn't want to think Melody just wanted to enjoy this moment, to feel what the music promised. She didn't want to be sad anymore.

The DJ played one last song which was slow. Collin took Melody into his arms. She relaxed as he held her close. She laid her head on his chest and closed her eyes. She let Collin mole her body into his and it was as if they were one. Collin thought, "How good she felt. How this is where she belonged, but she wasn't ready. Not ready to give herself, her whole self to him." He was determined to give her time. He didn't want to live in Juan's shadow............

When the song was over Collin continued to hold Melody. He looked down at her and she up at him. He smiled and then kissed her lightly on her lips. While the kiss was short and their lips barely touched they both felt a spark.

Collin said, "Thanks for coming out with me."

They left the club and headed to Melody's house. Collin and Melody were quiet throughout the ride. They both could feel the strong connection between them............. When they arrived at Melody's home Collin got out of the car and walked her to the front door. Melody opened the door.

"It was fun."

"Collin."

"Yes."

"Stay with me."

Collin gave Melody a questioning look." She smiled. "I don't want this night, this moment, to end. I don't want to be alone."

Collin seeing how vulnerable. He wanted to be cautious, but couldn't manage to leave her. He followed Melody into her house. Melody closed the door and locked it. She took him by the hand and led him into the living room.

"Would you like a drink?"

Collin smiled.

"What are you trying to do, get me drunk and have your way with me?"

"No!"

"I'm just kidding. Yes I'll have something."

Melody walked over to the bar.

"I had a good time tonight."

"So did I."

"I don't mean to take up your time."

"Don't worry about it. We're friends right?"

"Yes."

"Well that's what friends do. Besides I had a great time. I haven't been out in a while."

"Hey, where's your girlfriend?"

"I don't have one." Melody looked at him with suspicious eyes. "I don't. I have taken a few women out on occasion, but nothings going on with any of them."

As Collin sipped his drink Melody looked at Collin. She couldn't believe that she had not really looked at him before. Collin was six feet, one inch. He had a low cut fade, side burns, nicely trimmed mustache and goatee. His skin tone was golden brown. He was muscular, where you could see the bulge of his chest muscles through his shirt. He had a nice waist line and flat stomach. Melody figured that he probably had a six pack. She smiled to herself when she thought he even smelled nice. His smell turned her on. Collin caught her staring at him and saw the expression on her face. Collin smiled. He knew that look. When Melody noticed that Collin was looking at her she looked away embarrassed.

"Don't be embarrassed. You can check me out anytime you want."

"I was just wondering why no one has ever snatched you up."

"I had one serious relationship during college, but things didn't workout. Until now I hadn't found that special woman."

Melody looked at him curious. Still looking at him Melody sipped on her drink.

"You are a good dancer."

"So are you. So when are we going to do this again?"

"When would you like? Next Thursday they're open. I don't have any appointments on Friday."

"Oh. I can't. I suppose to meet with Davis."

Collin gave her a suspicious look.

"We are supposed to talk about selling Bill's house. He said that he could get me a good price."

"How long will that take?"

"Well he also asked me out to dinner."

"So you've considered it."

"Well."

"I apologize. You don't owe me any explanation. You should go out. You shouldn't just settle. You want to make sure that who you choose is the one."

"Thank you for being my friend."

Melody got up from the love seat and sat next to Collin on the couch. She laid her head on his shoulder. Collin lifted his arm and put it around Melody's shoulders. She rested her head on his chest. Melody closed her eyes. Melody drifted off to sleep. Collin placed their drinks on the side table and then leaned his head back. He caressed Melody's hair. He wondered if he should express his interest in her. Then he thought, "Maybe she only likes me as a friend. Maybe she is interested in this Davis character. Maybe she thinks it's too soon for any man."

A half hour later Collin fell asleep. Collin slept until eight thirty the next day. Melody was still asleep. Collin picked Melody up and carried her upstairs. He found the master suite. Collin entered the room. He walked over to the bed. He gently laid her onto the bed. Collin placed covers over her. Before leaving he looked down at her. He wanted so much to kiss her, but was afraid of waking her up. Collin blew a kiss at her. Melody stirred as if she felt it land on her lips.

Collin eased out of the room, walked down the hall and down the stairs. Collin left out of the house and got into his car. He started the car up. He sat outside of Melody's house for a few minutes and then pulled off.

As Collin drove home he debated whether to tell Melody that he was attracted to her. He weighed their current relationship. Collin didn't want to lose what they had.

When he arrived home Collin took a shower and then laid down. He fell asleep thinking about Melody...........................

Melody awakened two hours after Collin had gone. She looked around. Melody tried to recall the night before. She didn't remember going to bed. The last thing she remembered was resting her head on Collin's chest. She looked at the time. Melody got up and took a shower. When she came out of the shower she dressed in lounging wear. Melody was feeling better this morning. She called her mother and talked for a little while. Melody's mother was happy that she sounded better.

After Melody hung up with her mother she called Collin. The phone rang twice. Collin answered the phone.

"Hello."

"Hi Collin."

"Hi. Did you get a good night's sleep?"

"Yes. Better than I have in a long time. Collin I have a question to ask you."

"What is it?"

"Was I in my bed before you left?"

"Yes."

"When did I go up there?"

"You didn't. When I got ready to leave I carried you up to your room and placed you in bed. I didn't want to leave you on the couch."

"Thank you. You are so sweet. Are you still coming over tomorrow?"

"Yes."

"Come over early. We can hang out. I'm going to church. I should be back by two."

"Okay. I'll be there at three."

Melody hung up the phone. She cleaned up her house. Melody prepared her clothes for church. Later she fixed herself a light salad. She was in bed by ten.

Chapter 9

The next morning Melody awakened early. She took food out for dinner. Melody looked around the downstairs to make sure everything was clean.

After doing so she left for church. As Melody drove to church she thought of her life. She thought of her marriage to Bill and how in the beginning of their relationship and marriage there were some happy times. She thanked God for those times. Melody thought of the bad times with Bill. They out weighed the good times.

Her mind went to Juan. She thought of the times when he flirted with her. Melody smiled.

Then she thought of how he saved her life and helped her through her divorce. Melody got a warm feeling.

When she arrived at church Melody parked her car and then headed inside. As the minister preached Melody felt as if he was talking directly to her.

When he was finished with his sermon and the service came to an end Melody got out of her seat. As she was leaving the minister stopped her. He asked her how she was doing and said that he was happy to see her in service. He hugged Melody and blessed her. Melody thanked the minister, purchased a cd and then left.

As she drove home Melody listened to the cd...............

When Melody arrived home she changed clothes and then began cooking. She prepared some finger foods for her and Collin to eat before dinner.

The doorbell rang at three o'clock. Melody went to answer it. When she opened the door Collin was standing there with a bouquet of flowers and a bottle of wine. Melody reached out, hugged and lightly kissed him on the lips. Collin handed her the flowers and wine.

"Come in. I made some refreshments while dinner is still cooking. Would you like some?"

Collin followed her into the kitchen. He took a few of the snacks.

"These are good."

"Have a seat."

Melody sat the wine to chill.

"So, I have this money from Bill. I would like to donate some of it to a charity. Which charity do you propose I give it to?"

"Are there any groups that you feel strong about?"

Melody thought about the question.

"There are a few, but I don't know. I want the money to really count for something."

Collin sat back and was quiet for a while. He looked at Melody and tried to think of how to phrase his words gently.

"Melody I really don't know how to say this gently. How about donating to a charity for battered women."

Melody looked at Collin. She was quiet. Melody checked on her meal.

"You know I thought of that, but I wanted to do something on a much larger scale. I want to make sure that the help is actually going directly to the people."

"What you can do is think about what battered people need and want. Don't they need clothing for themselves and for their children? The children may need supplies for school. They need help with transportation. Also you can contact centers and talk to them."

"That's a good idea. I'll start calling places tomorrow."

"I will look into some things as well. We have students who have privately come to the administration through some of the agencies."

Melody took the meat out of the oven. She placed the dish on the stove. Melody opened the wine and poured some in two crystal goblets. She handed one to Collin. He took it and sipped some before placing the goblet down. Melody also sipped some of the liquid before placing it down.

"This is good."

Melody fixed their plates and then handed Collin's his. Collin thought how that she must have made a great wife.

As they ate Melody and Collin continued to discuss plans to donate some of her money. When they were finished eating Collin helped Melody clean the kitchen. They took the rest of the wine and goblets into the living room. As it got late Collin said, "I think I better be going. I have an early morning."

"Are you sure you can drive, you've had a few drinks."

Collin thought about it.

"I'll be alright."

"Collin stay here tonight. You can get up early, go home and change." Collin looked at her. "You can stay in the guess room."

"Are you sure?"

"Yes. I don't want to cause anymore accidents. I don't want anyone else to die because of me."

Collin looked at Melody curiously.

"Melody do you think that it's your fault that Bill, Juan and Juanita died?" Melody looked down. Collin walked over to the love seat and sat next to Melody. He placed his hand under her chin. He lifted her chin. Melody looked into his eyes. He noticed sadness and thought, "How could such beautiful eyes be so sad all the time?"

He then spoke, "You didn't cause Bill to abuse you. You didn't cause him to ram his car into Juan's car. Bill did all of this. He was mentally ill and he took your family's lives. Don't take this into yourself. All these things have happened to you, not because of you. They are unfortunate events, but you have survived. You are a survivor." Collin lightly kissed Melody on the lips. Melody closed her eyes. She placed her arms around his neck and laid her head on him. Collin held her. After an hour Melody stopped crying.

"I'm sorry."

"There's nothing to be sorry about. I'm happy to be here for you."

Melody got up and took Collin's hand.

"Collin come upstairs so you can get some sleep." Melody led him up to the guest room. "You can sleep in here. There are towels in the bathroom." Melody kissed him lightly on the lips. "Good night."

"Good night."

Collin went into the room and got into bed. Collin laid in bed thinking about Melody. His mind recalled kissing Melody. Then he thought of when Melody kissed him. "Could this mean that she is feeling me? Am I reading more into this then there is?" Collin drifted off to sleep.............................

Melody laid awake thinking of Collin's touch and the spark that she felt when he kissed her. "Can he have feelings for me? Am I reading more into this than there is? Maybe he wants to take it slow." Melody smiled to herself. She thought of how up front Juan was with her. She knew where she stood with him. Melody thought of Davis, how he was up front with letting her know that he was interested. He was good looking. Melody was hesitant because she didn't know whether he just wanted to sleep with her because of something Bill had told him or wanted a relationship. Melody soon drifted off to sleep......................................

Melody began dreaming: *She and Collin was on a date. They had gone to a club. A slow song was playing and Collin held her close. The two danced to a few songs. Melody saw a man come up behind Collin. The man tapped Collin on the shoulder. The man said, "Can I cut in?" Collin looked at Melody. She looked at him with a devilish eye and then nodded her head yes. Collin bent down and kissed the side of her face. He ran his hand down the side of her face. The other man took Melody into his arms and they began to slow dance. The man whispered, "You look beautiful. Melody looked at him and realized that it was Davis.*

Melody asked, "What are you doing here?"

"I'm here for you."

"Why?"

"Because you need me."

Davis spin Melody around and then dipped her. They continued dancing. The scene changed and Melody was in a

146

man's bedroom. She was kissing the man. She opened her eyes and it was Collin. Collin picked her up and carried her over to the bed. He laid her down onto the bed. Collin sat next to her. Just as he bent down to kiss Melody he felt a tap on his shoulder. Melody looked. It was Davis.

Davis said, "Can I cut in?"

Collin looked at Davis.

"No, you may not cut in. Why are you here?"

"She wants me here."

Collin looked at Melody. Melody shook her head in disagreement.

"I disagree."

"Yes you did. Look if you didn't ask for me here, why am I?"

Collin looked at Melody. He got off of the bed. He moved back.

"Where are you going?"

Collin continued to move back. Davis sat on the bed. Melody looked for Collin. He continued to move back until he disappeared. Davis cupped her face.

"Don't worry about him. I'm here."

Davis bent down to kiss Melody.

Just as he went to kiss her Melody awakened. She looked at the clock. It was six o'clock. She got out of bed. As she walked into the bathroom Melody remembered that Collin had spent the night. She left the bathroom and went to the guest room.

When Melody got there the door was open. Melody cautiously walked in. The bed was made. Melody called out, but there wasn't any answer. She looked around the room. She went downstairs and walked through the house. There was no sign that Collin had ever been there. Melody went into the kitchen and fixed herself breakfast..............

As she ate Melody thought of her dream and tried to figure out if it meant anything. Then Melody thought of their night out and how he had held her, so familiar, so close. Melody felt warm as she thought about it. Melody finished eating and then straightened up her house..........

After ten she called one of the shelters. Melody was happy that she was able to get a number of places to think about................

Collin called Melody later in the day and gave her more names and ideas.

Thursday morning Collin asked Melody what she had planned for the evening. Melody reminded him of her meeting with Davis. Collin was silent for a while.

"Be careful."

Melody thought it was sweet how he tried to seem concerned, but was obviously jealous.

"I will."

Melody hung up the phone.....

All week Melody had contemplated her meeting with Davis. She wondered if he would be pushy or low key, which didn't seem to be his character. Davis called Melody to make sure they were still on. Melody told him that she would be at his office at three o'clock. He inquired about her decision to go out to dinner. Melody paused trying to act as if she had not thought of the invite.

Finally she agreed to accompany him.

After getting off the phone Melody looked into her closet and found a business suit that was also appropriate for dinner.

At two thirty Melody left her home. She drove to Davis' office. A half hour later she arrived outside of his office. She looked in her over head mirror to check her hair. Melody exited the car and straightened her clothes. She then went into the building. Melody gave her name to the receptionist. Melody noticed the look that the receptionist gave her. As Davis came out almost immediately, he took Melody's hand and kissed her on the side of her face. The receptionist's look was almost envious. Melody and Davis walked into his office and he closed the door behind him.

"How are you gorgeous?"

"I'm fine. How about yourself?"

"I'm great now."

"Davis, I mean Larry, have you talked with your contact?"

"Davis is fine. I like the way you say it. I talked to my associate and he gave me a lead to a top realtor. I called her, a Ms. Parks. She said that she could meet you on Saturday. About one. Is that good for you?"

"Yes. I guess I'll go by the house tomorrow to see what it looks like."

"You haven't been by there since I gave you the keys?"

"No."

"Would you like me to go with you?"

Melody looked at him surprised.

"You wouldn't mind?"

"I told you I would like to spend time with you."

"I don't think that this is what you had in mind."

"Well if I'm going to get to know you I have to start somewhere." Melody looked at him in a questioning way. "I'm serious. I want to get to know you. Bill told me a lot about you." Melody face turned from questioning to fear. "He didn't tell me anything personal like what you two did intimately. He just told me that you were beautiful. He was right. Actually I think he held back on describing the way you look. He said that you were sweet and kind. I can see that. He said that you were perfect and a devoted wife and that he screwed up. That's why he wanted to leave you everything he had. He said that he knew he could never make up for how he treated you and what he's done to you, but maybe in this small way he could show you that he regretted all of it. You know he told me that he was sick inside and he couldn't take not having you. He said having you made him whole, but there were times that he couldn't control himself." Davis became quiet for a few minutes. "Enough of that you're trying to move on with your life and I'm trying to be a part of that move. Are you hungry?"

"I could stand to eat something."

Davis took her by the arm.

"Well let's go."

Davis and Melody left out of his office. Melody noticed the same expression as before on the receptionist's face. As they were leaving Davis told his secretary that he would not be returning. The secretary said, "Good night."

Davis and Melody walked to the same restaurant that they had gone to on their first outing.

The two ordered drinks and their meal. As they sipped on their drinks Melody and Davis shared some of their life experiences....................

When the meal was brought to them they ordered another drink. Melody and Davis talked for several hours.......................

After leaving the restaurant Davis walked Melody to her car. They talked in front of her car for a while.

After some time Davis helped Melody into her car. Before closing the door Davis kissed Melody on the side of her face. He asked her out again. They made arrangements to have a date the next Thursday...........................

When Melody got home she noticed a message waiting on her phone. She checked the message. It was Collin. He had just hung up. Melody changed clothes and then called Collin. His phone rang twice."

"Hello."

"Hi, it's Melody."

"Hi Melody. I just called to check on you."

"I'm fine. I just got home a few minutes ago. I checked my messages. "What's up?"

"I was wondering what you were doing tomorrow night."

"I don't have any plans. Why?"

"Would you like to go dancing?"

"Sure!"

Collin noticed the excitement in Melody's voice and was happy for it.

"Ok. I'll come by your house and pick you up at five. We can go out to eat and then head to the club, if that's alright."

"Yes that would be fine."

Melody and Collin talked a little while longer before hanging up. She told him about her and Davis meeting with the realtor. Collin offered his assistance and Melody thanked him. She felt bad not accepting his offer. She knew spending time with Davis bothered Collin. Melody wasn't sure if it was a man thing, he didn't like Davis or if it was because he was jealous of he being interested in her. Melody didn't understand why he didn't just come out and tell her. Then Melody thought how she would handle it. Melody wondered if she was ready to date. Collin noticed the silence. He told her that he would see her tomorrow and wished her a good rest.

That night Melody stayed up late thinking about these two new men in her life. She knew Davis intentions, but wasn't sure of Collin's. Sometimes he would lead her to think that he was interested in her romantically, but then he would say something to leave her to believe he was just interested in being her friend. Melody thought of her feelings about both men. While she was intrigued with Davis, she actually liked Collin a lot. Davis was about six feet tall. He was criminally attractive. Davis had deep dimples in his cheeks and one in his chin. His eyes were light brown. He was light skinned. Davis wore thin side burns and had no other facial hair. He wore a close hair cut. His suits fit his body as if tailored made. Davis has a deep sexy voice. She actually enjoyed talking with him. He was very interesting. Collin was not only good looking, he was charming. She thought that Collin was not only charming, she felt that he was sincere in wanting to help her move on with her life. She didn't feel that he was seeking to get anything from her. Melody felt secure and protected when she was with Collin. She wasn't sure how she felt about Davis. Melody wondered if his interest was strictly physical. Melody drifted off to sleep comparing the two men.

Second Chances

Chapter 10

Melody began to dream:

"She was at a club. Melody was sitting alone at a table. Davis walked up and asked her for a dance. He held his hand out. As she went to take it Collin walked up. He held his hand out. She looked at both men. She couldn't decide which hand to take. Melody just sat there looking at these two handsome men. She went to reach for Collin's hand, but Davis took her hand and pulled her up to him. They began dancing.

Davis asked, "Why did you hesitate? I can make you happy. I'm the best man for you."

Melody didn't say anything. She looked back and Collin was still standing where they had left him.

156

After a few dances Collin tapped Davis on the shoulder. Davis looked back. For a second Davis just looked at Collin. He kissed Melody on the side of her face and then gave her hand to Collin. Collin took Melody into his arms. Melody laid her head on Collin's chest. They danced to several songs. Collin looked down at Melody. He asked, "Would you like to leave?" Melody shook her head in agreement. He took her by the hand.

As they walked the scenery changed. They were walking along the beach. The water rushed up close to them. Melody could feel the cool breeze of the ocean. Collin put his arm around her shoulders. She leaned her head on him as they continued to walk. Collin stopped. He pulled her close to him. She went willingly into his arms. He lifted her head. He bent down and lightly kissed her lips. It was short. Melody tasted the salt of the mist coming from off the ocean. He bent and kissed her again. This time lingering. She placed her arms around his waist. He pressed her closer to him. As they kissed the scene changed again. They were no longer on the beach. They were in her bedroom. Collin picked Melody up and carried her to the bed. He laid her on the bed. Melody looked up at Collin.

Melody asked, "Should we be here?"

Collin responded, "What do you think?"

Melody closed her eyes. She thought about the question, "Am I ready for this? Am I moving too soon? What about my marriage?

Melody awakened. She looked around the room. Melody realized it was all a dream. She laid there thinking about the dream. "Am I moving too fast? Should I ask Collin if he is interested? Would that mean that I'm being naive? I would feel embarrassed if he's not interested romantically and then it may make him uncomfortable."

Melody got up, showered and then got dressed. She had to drop her paper off and then she had the rest of the day to herself. Melody decided to go shopping for a new dress to go out with her friend. She looked at the beautiful dresses. Melody wanted to look nice, but not overly dressed.

After selecting a dress, shoes and a matching purse Melody went to get a manicure and pedicure. Although it was fall, it was still rather warm. Melody went home. She didn't want to be starved when Collin gets there.

Melody fixed a salad and steamed some shrimp to put on it. She remembered Juan telling her to stop starving herself. Melody sat down and ate her salad. She then went up to her room and showered.

Melody began to get dressed. She sprayed perfume over her body. Melody sprayed perfume over her head, behind her ears, wrist and ankles. She then put her stockings on. Even though she didn't plan on anyone seeing them Melody always felt sexy wearing them. She clipped them onto her garter. Melody smoothed the stockings and she put on her dress. She beveled her hair and then put on her shoes.

Melody looked at herself in the mirror. She approved of her look and then put some lip stick on and a little eye shadow. Melody heard the ringing of her door bell. She quickly changed over her purse and then ran down the stairs. She opened the door. Collin stood quiet for a few minutes before saying anything. She could tell that he approved of her look. The way he was looking at her made her face flush. Collin noticed. He leaned over and kissed her lightly on the lips.

"You look beautiful."

"Thank you."

"Are you ready?"

"Yes."

Melody stepped out of the house. She closed the front door and they walked to his car. Collin opened the car door for Melody. She entered the car. Collin closed the door behind her. He got into the car and drove off. Collin drove to a Mexican Restaurant. When they arrived he parked the car. As they walked to the entrance Collin placed his hand behind Melody's back. It felt natural to her. He opened the door of the restaurant and Melody walked in. They were quickly seated. Melody ordered a volcano and the two shared it. They ordered their food. Melody and Collin talked about their week. Melody noticed that he looked at her differently tonight. It made her feel desirable. As they ate Melody talked about her plans when she finishes school. Melody confided that she would like to open up her own practice.

When they were finished with their meal the two left the restaurant and headed to the club. Melody looked out into the night's air.

"What are you thinking?"

"Nothing really. I love to look at the lighted buildings at night. The night looks so enchanting."

"So do you."

Melody looked at him. Collin looked at her with a devilish smile. Melody blushed.

When they arrived at the club Collin parked the car. As they walked to the club's door Collin placed his arm around Melody's waist. They walked into the club.

"Do you want to dance or sit down and have a drink?"

"I would like to dance with you."

Collin looked at her questioning. Collin hand was still behind her. He guided her to the dance floor. Collin took her by the hand and spin her around.

After they had danced to several songs Collin took Melody by the hand and led her to the bar. He ordered drinks for the two of them. Melody took her drink and then put her arm around Collin's arm. He was happy that she felt comfortable enough to do it. They sat down at a near by seat.

As they sipped their drinks Melody and Collin looked on as couples danced. When they were rested Collin pulled Melody onto her feet and they began dancing again. After several fast dances the DJ announced that he was slowing the music down. Collin pulled Melody close. She placed her arms around his neck. As they danced to the music Melody rested her head on his chest. Collin held her close. Collin kissed Melody on the top of head. Collin felt Melody's arms tighten around him. He whispered, "Your smell is driving me crazy."

They continued to dance. When the music turned fast again Melody and Collin stayed locked in each other's arms. They stayed with the rhythm of the music. The two danced until the club closed.

Melody and Collin were both quiet as they drove back to her house.

When they arrived at Melody's house Collin got out of the car and walked her to the door. He bent down and kissed Melody lightly on the lips.

"Thank you for the dance."

"Thank you for taking me."

Collin turned to leave. Melody grabbed his hand to stop him. "Are you ready for the night to end?"

"Not really."

"Would you like to come in and keep me company?"

Collin turned. Melody unlocked the door and they walked into the house. "Would you like a drink?"

"Sure."

Melody went to get them drinks. She made two drinks and brought them back to the living room. Melody handed Collin his drink. He thanked her and sipped on it. Melody turned on soft music.

"Melody I've been meaning to tell you something all night."

"What is it? Dance with me."

Collin stood up and held his hand out to her. Melody took his hand. He spin her around and then pulled her to him. "You know you are a good dancer."

"I think you are a good dancer as well. I just follow your lead."

Collin pulled her even closer.

"Melody I have something to tell you."

Melody stopped moving.

"What is it?"

"I have to go away. I'll be away for two weeks." Melody looked at him. "There is a conference in Europe. The college is sending me. I may be away a month."

"Do you have to go? I'm sorry. I have no right to ask you that. I've just gotten use to having you around. I mean I feel somehow protected with you around. Not that I need protecting. I like you around."

"I didn't realize. This is a privilege to go to this conference and meet with other Psychiatrist." Collin lifted her chin. "I'll always be here for you."

Melody bent down and took their glasses. She made them another drink. She handed him his drink and drank from hers. They sat quiet. Melody continued to sip on her drink until she was finished. She made another for herself. As she sipped it tears ran down her face. Collin looked at her. He saw the tears. He tried to compose himself. This woman was in his blood. He knew if he tried to console her he would lose himself. He remained still. Collin took a drink of the liquid.

"Melody I didn't mean to make you sad."

"You didn't. I don't mean to spoil your night. I'm being selfish. I've gotten use to you being around. This is your moment in life. Who am I to ask you to stop your life? I'm just a sad woman with a lot of problems. You have been such a good friend to me."

"You have been through a lot. You may be feeling sad, but you're not sad. You are a smart, beautiful sexy woman. I'll be away for a month, but then I'll be back. I'll call you when I can."

"When are you leaving?"

"Monday."

"I know this may be selfish of me, but I don't want to be alone. I'll be alone while you're gone."

"You'll have Davis."

Melody looked at Collin and saw the jealous look on his face.

"We have more than what I have with Davis. Davis is helping me sale Bill's house."

"I care about you too."

Melody went and made herself another drink.

"Stay with me until Sunday. I know you have to pack."

Collin gave her a questioning look.

"Are you afraid that I'm not coming back?"

The look on Melody's face gave him his answer. Collin couldn't restrain himself any longer. He walked over to her. Collin held her. Melody put her face in his chest. He held her hair and kissed her on the forehead. He held his lips to her head. Collin wrapped both of his arms around Melody's shoulders. "I'll stay." Melody wrapped her arms around his waist.

"I think you need to lay down."

"I'll see you in the morning?"

"Yes. I'll be in the guest room."

"Can you lay next to me in my bed, just until I fall asleep?"

Collin looked at her. He didn't think it was wise, but Collin couldn't say no to this woman. He let her lead him to her room.

When they entered her room Melody asked if he mind her taking a shower. He lied and said no. He pulled the covers back as she went into the bathroom. Collin laid down. He lay there knowing Melody was just a few steps away necked. He felt himself getting aroused and scold himself. He closed his eyes and thought of their dance and how she felt in his arms. Collin thought of her smell. Collin heard the bathroom door open. He opened his eyes. Melody was dressed in a long black silk night gown. It was low cut with lace around the chest and bottom of it. The gown fitted every curve.

As she walked over to the bed it was as if time had slowed. Melody hair was out. It laid over her shoulders. Collin asked himself how was he going to compose himself. He watched every step with her getting closer. When she finally made it over to the bed Melody laid next to Collin. He put his arm behind her head and laid on his back. Melody turned side ways and rested her head on his chest.

"You can't be comfortable."

"I'm fine."

"Take that shirt off. You have a t-shirt on. Come on get comfortable."

Collin took off his shirt. He laid back down. Melody laid her head on his chest. She then placed her hand on his chest. Collin thought to himself, "Does this woman realize the torture she is putting me through?"

Melody shifted.

"Collin."

"Yes."

"Hold me."

Collin obeyed. He placed his free arm around Melody. Collin continued to lay on his back. He held Melody's body close to his. He caressed her back.

"Collin."

"Yes."

"Are you attracted to me?"

"Are you kidding? You are a beautiful woman. Any man would have to be blind not to find you attractive."

Collin kissed Melody on her forehead.

"Collin kiss me."

"I just did."

"No for real."

"Are you sure?" Collin remembered there first kiss, how sensual it was.

"Collin please."

"Melody are you sure?"

"Please. I need you to kiss me. Please."

Collin sat up. Melody laid her head on her pillow. Collin looked down at her. He thought, "You are so beautiful." He took her hands and pulled her up to him. He placed his hands on both sides of her face. He leaned closer and gently kissed her. He looked at Melody. He saw loneliness in her eyes. Collin moved his hands to her arms and then kissed her again. As they kissed he squeezed her arms. As the kiss became more intense Collin wrapped one arm around Melody's waist. He held her head with the other hand. Melody wrapped her arms around his neck. She held his head. Collin kissed her forehead. He kissed her nose, the side of her face and moved to her neck. While Collin kissed Melody's neck she whispered, "I miss this." Collin stopped and looked into Melody's eyes. He saw passion. He knew there was no turning back. He didn't want to turn back. Collin put his hand under Melody's chin.

"Gorgeous are you sure this is what you want?"

Melody looked into his eyes. Collin saw loneliness, sadness and desire. He wanted to fill her loneliness, take away her sadness and fulfill her desire. Collin took her into his arms and kissed her. Melody wrapped her arms around Collins neck. He pulled her to him. Collin took Melody on a journey where sadness was not known and loneliness was replaced with fulfillment. Melody's desire was matched with Collin's.....................

The next morning Melody woke up in Collin's arms. She nestled closer. Collin tightened his grip. Melody thought how wonderful it felt being held. She kissed Collin on the lips. She smoothed her hand over his face. Melody closed her eyes. She fell back to sleep.

Collin awakened. He saw that Melody was still laying on his chest. Collin ran his hand down Melody's arm. She nestled closer. Collin kissed Melody on the forehead and then eased out of bed. Collin went into the guest room and took a shower. He put his pants on and then went downstairs. He called in an order for lunch.

While he waited Collin sat on the couch and thought about the night before. He could never have imagined that what they did would have happened. Collin wondered if he should have been stronger, that maybe they should have waited. It had been a long time since he had been with a woman and there was something about this woman that he couldn't deny anything. At that moment she desired him and it was a turn on. He wanted Melody to be in his world and wanted to be the man that she dreamed of. Collin sat hoping that he had not messed things up between them by him not being able to say no to her...........

When the food arrived Collin placed it on plates. He placed the plates on trays and took the food up to Melody's room.

When he entered the room he heard the shower going and noticed that Melody had gotten up. Collin thought of going to join her, but wasn't sure where they stood. Collin placed the trays down. He sat on a chair not far from the bed and waited for Melody to come out of the bathroom.

Collin thought of her being in the shower and how good her body felt just a few hours earlier. He smiled thinking of how he would have never thought her to make love to him the way she had. Collin could see how Bill had not wanted to let her go. He wondered if she had been the same way with Bill. Collin liked to think that he had brought it out in her.

When Melody came out of the bathroom her eyes lit up. She walked over to Collin. He put his arms around her waist. Melody put her arms around his neck.

"I thought you had left."

"You asked me to stay until Sunday."

"I know, but I didn't know how you felt this morning."

"I feel the way I've been feeling for a long time."

"What do you mean?"

"I don't know if I should say. How do you feel about last night?"

"Don't feel obligated."

"I'm not understanding."

"Collin I'm falling in love with you. I know you just wanted us to just be friends."

Collin looked at Melody in disbelief.

"I do want to be your friend, but that's not all. I didn't think that you were ready for anything more than friendship."

"I don't know what's going on with me. I feel alone most of the time. When I'm with you I don't feel alone. Do you think that I'm moving too fast? Should I be doing this, feeling like I do about you? Do you think bad of me?"

"Why should I think bad of you?"

"Because it's only been a short while since my husband died and now I've slept with you and I have these feelings."

"No, I don't feel bad of you. No one can tell you when you are ready to move on, to live again. I feel honored that you care for me. I'm just not sure if what you feel is not gratitude. Don't think bad of me for saying what I'm about to say. Melody I think that you should go out with this Davis guy while I'm away. If when I come back you want a relationship with me than I'll know that what you say you feel is true."

"Collin I don't want to lose you."

"You won't. No matter what happens I will be your friend and I will always be here for you."

Collin smoothed his hand along the side of Melody's face. Melody placed her hand on his. She placed his hand to her mouth and kissed it. Melody then placed his arm around her waist. Collin lifted her up. She wrapped her legs around his waist. Collin kissed her. Melody removed the towel from around herself. Collin took in her fragrance. Melody held onto Collin. They kissed. Collin held onto Melody as he removed his pants. Their desire heightened. Their passion rose to unimaginable heights. Collin had made love to women before, but nothing matched how she made him feel. Melody still seemed innocent. He was turned on by her not being inhibited. He made love to this woman forgetting about the world or the food that sat on the dresser getting cold.

After their bodies had given way to their pleasure Collin moved over to the bed and eased Melody onto it. They laid in each other's arms. Melody and Collin fell asleep...............................

Melody awakened first. She kissed Collin's cheek and then smoothed her hand over his chest. Melody laid there thinking of their conversation. She caressed his chest. She whispered, careful not to wake Collin. "I am in love with you. I'll do as you say. I hope you will want me as much as I want to be with you when you get back."

Collin heard what Melody said. He pretended to sleep. He wanted to take back what he had said just a little while ago, but he truly wanted Melody or maybe he was the one that needed to be sure that he is what she wanted.

Melody eased out of bed. She noticed the food on the dresser. Melody took a peace of the fruit and ate it on the way to the bathroom. While Melody was in the bathroom Collin got up, went downstairs and heated up the food.

When he came back up he heard the shower. He placed the food down and then went into the bathroom. He walked slowly towards the shower watching Melody. He opened up the shower door. Melody smiled. "I was hoping you would join me."

Collin stepped into the shower. Melody picked up the bath sponge, put shower gel on it and commence to washing Collin's body.

Collin thought to himself, "I could get use to this. How could I think of sending her to another man?"

When Melody had finished washing Collin's body he in term washed hers'. The way he touched her sent sparks throughout Melody's body. Melody thought, "This man has no idea what he does to me each time that he touch me. I've never felt this way before. How can I have had two husbands and never felt what Collin make me feel? "Melody wrapped her arms around Collin and kissed him.

"Don't start anything. We haven't eaten in a day."

"Who needs to eat food?"

"We do. Come on. I heated the food up."

"If you insist."

"I do."

Melody looked at Collin and smiled. She thought to herself, "I hope so."

Collin read her mind, "When I come back."

"What?"

"Nothing."

They finished drying off. Melody put a robe on and Collin put his pants back on. They sat on the love seat in Melody's bedroom and ate. Throughout the meal Melody glanced at Collin's body. She thought of how nice his body was, how his arms were so strong and she loved when he held her. Thinking about how he held her while they made love turned her on. When Collin looked at her he could see the desire in her eyes.

Collin asked, "Melody?"

When she looked at Collin, he could see the passion in her eyes. He had to look away to concentrate.

"Yes."

"Were you always this passionate?"

"You may not believe this, but no."

Collin looked at her in a questioning manner.

"Really? Why me?"

"I didn't know that I even had passion. You bring it out."

Collin ran his finger down her leg. Collin watched Melody's face. He got on his knees in front of her. He placed his hand behind her head. He brought it closer to him. He kissed her passionately. He pulled her onto the floor with him. They stayed on their knees kissing. They couldn't get enough of each other. Neither wanted this moment in their lives to end...............................

The next morning came in quicker than the couple wanted. The sun shined bright through the bedroom curtains. Melody awakened. Although she welcomed the beauty of the sun, Melody knew the wonderful experience that she had with Collin was over. She wondered if he would come back to her or if he would feel what he felt this weekend. She wondered if Collin didn't want a relationship with her would she ever feel what she felt this wonderful weekend. Melody held Collin tighter. Collin felt her and tightened his grip on her. They both held onto each other knowing that last night was over and this moment in their lives were soon coming to an end.

"Collin will you call me while you're away?"

"I'll call you every chance I get. Even when we're not talking you will be on my mind."

Melody reluctantly got up. They took their shower together. Both were quiet. They took turns washing each other. His hands drove her crazy. Each touch was maddening until she couldn't resist. She looked at him and Collin knew that he couldn't resist. He picked her up. She held onto him as if in desperation. What they felt blocked out where they were. As Collin squeezed her body to his Melody whispered "I love you."

Melody and Collin dressed and then went downstairs. Melody cooked them breakfast. When they sat down to eat Melody said a prayer. She thanked God for their food and asked him to watch over Collin while he was away and to bring him back safely. They ate in silence.

When they had finished eating Collin helped her with the dishes. Melody asked him to stay and she would cook him dinner, but Collin regretfully told her that he had to get home, change clothes (they laughed) and pack for his trip. Melody walked Collin to the door. He took her hands and brought them up to his lips. He kissed them. Collin then took her hands and put them behind him. He pulled her close to him and kissed her. It started out a gentle goodbye kiss which turned into passion. When he felt himself loosing control Collin pulled away. "I better go. I'll call you." Collin kissed Melody on the nose.

After Collin left Melody locked her front door. She surveyed her downstairs and then went up to her bedroom. She cleaned her bedroom and bathroom. Melody laid down. She thought of her weekend with Collin and the things that he had told her. Melody wondered if she had fallen in love with a man who didn't love her back. She thought, "Am I just feeling grateful? Am I feeling this way because I feel alone? Did my body respond that way because it's been a while since it's been touched? I guess Collin was being nice. I guess he slept with me because men have needs. I can't believe that he would have made love to me the way he did if he didn't care just a little." Melody drifted off to sleep. Melody tossed and turned throughout the night. Although it had been a short time Melody had come accustomed to being in Collin's arms.

When Collin arrived home he changed into lounging clothes. He pulled out a suit bag. Collin took several suits out and placed them in the bag. When he was finished packing Collin checked his flight on his laptop. He then placed the laptop in his bag. Collin laid down. As Collin laid there he thought about his time with Melody. His mind went back to the first night where they sat on the couch and Melody fell asleep in his arms. He remembered her scent and how it aroused him. He recalled the first time Melody kissed him. He had longed for her to kiss him like that again and be aware of it and not be in a dilemma. Their weekend she had kissed him with such passion he could not think beyond that moment. She had made love to him like one who was in love. He wasn't sure if she was in love with him or just lonely. Could this woman be in love with him or trying to fill her emptiness. He couldn't believe that he had put his heart out only to be broken.

Collin tossed and turned throughout the night. He missed Melody being in his arms.

After some time passed Collin finally fell asleep.....................

Two hours later the alarm went off and it was time for him to get up. Collin got up, showered and then got dressed. He took his luggage, laptop and left for the airport.

After checking in and going through security Collin sat down and drifted off to sleep..........

It was an hour later when the airline began calling passengers. Collin got up and stood in line. He boarded the plan and as quickly as he was seated fell asleep..................

When he awakened the flight was on its way and they were serving breakfast. Collin drank his coffee and ate the fruit. He thought about his weekend. He didn't realize how tired he was. He hadn't gotten much sleep throughout the weekend. Collin smiled thinking about it.

After he had finished his coffee and fruit Collin fell back to sleep.....................

Melody awakened to the sound of the alarm clock. She laid there a few minutes before getting up. Melody was tired from the weekend and restless night. She smiled thinking of the weekend. Melody got up, and dressed. She had a long day. She missed Collin already. She thought of how different the school would be since Collin wouldn't be there. Melody left her home and headed to the campus.

When Melody arrived at the college, force of habit she went to Collin's office and then realized that he wasn't there.....................

Melody felt a lost but got through the day.

Melody got through the week keeping busy. Although she had second thoughts about going out with Davis she actually welcomed the distraction.

When Davis picked her up at home he kissed her on the side of her face. Melody couldn't believe how different it felt. Before her weekend with Collin she was somewhat attracted to Davis. Now being with him was just going through the motion. She felt bad and contemplated asking him to take her back home, but she remembered what Collin had told her and decided to go forward with the date.

Davis' charms closed her mind of Collin. He kept her attention and made her laugh throughout dinner.

After dinner Davis asked Melody if she wanted to go out dancing. Melody told him that she wasn't up for dancing. Davis paid for dinner and they left the restaurant. Davis took Melody by her hand and walked across the street to the park that was adjacent to the restaurant. It was a warm night in November. They walked a while not saying anything, just taking in the scenery. Melody didn't want to, but she had to admit it was nice walking in the warm night air. She always loved the park and this park was lit up with white lights and had beautiful fall flowers. In one area it was dressed in pink and white mums. There was a Gazebo. Davis stepped in it first. Melody stepped in after. There was soft music coming from the restaurant. Davis did not ask. He pulled Melody to him and swayed to the music. At first Melody felt uneasy. Melody felt as if she was betraying Collin. Then she heard a lyric from the music saying. "When a man loves a woman." Melody relaxed. Davis held her closer. Melody laid her head on his shoulder and closed her eyes. A car drove by and beeped it's horn. It broke the spell of the music and Melody jumped.

"I guess we better go."

"I think so."

Davis took Melody by the hand and led her back to his car. Melody and Davis entered the car. As he drove back to Melody's house Davis made light conversation.

When they arrived in front of her house Davis parked. Melody immediately went for the door. Davis reached over.

"Melody can I get a good night's kiss?"

Melody was hesitant. She knew what Collin had said, but she had reservations. She turned and allowed Davis to kiss her. "Is that the best you can do? Why are you holding back? It's only a kiss." Melody placed one hand on the side of Davis' face and leaned closer. She kissed him lightly. Davis put his hand behind her head. He returned her kiss with such passion that it left Melody's head reeling. Melody pulled away and looked at Davis.

"I think I better go in."

"How about next week? We'll go dancing."

Melody thought about it. She liked dancing. She recalled Collin's words and decided to take Davis up on his offer. Melody thought to herself, "What could it hurt? I need something to get me through until Collin gets back.

"Sure."

"Ok. I'll pick you up Thursday at six. We'll get something to eat and then go dancing." Davis kissed her lightly on the lips. "See you next week."

Melody went into the house. She looked around the house, where it had once been filled with life, it was now empty. Melody's concentration was broken by the ringing of the phone. Melody picked it up.

"Hello."

"Hey I forgot. We have to go to the house tomorrow."

Melody was quiet for a moment.

"Oh, right. I forgot. I'll meet you there."

"Is twelve o'clock good?"

"Yes that will be fine. I'll see you then."

Melody hung up the phone. She went up to her room. For a moment Melody thought she smelled Collin's cologne. She looked around the room. She scolded herself. She knew she was supposed to give that relationship a brake. Then she questioned if it was a relationship. Melody got ready for bed. She laid down and quickly fell asleep...............

The next morning Melody awakened early. She got dressed and left to go to Bill's house. She was kind of nervous. She wished that Collin was here to go with her. Melody had not been there in over five years. She parked in front of the house. Melody sat there a few minutes trying to conjure up the courage to enter alone. She told herself, "Well you're here. You came early because you wanted to finally face your fear."

Melody got out of the car. She went up to the front door. She stood and stared at it for a while.

Finally Melody, as if in slow motion put the key into the lock and turned it. The door opened. At first Melody just stood looking as if waiting for Bill to show up. Melody walked into the house and closed the door. The house was stuffy. Melody walked into the living room. As she walked toward the window to open it, Melody stopped. As if watching a scene from a movie, she had a flash back:

"Melody looked at this mantle." Melody looked toward the mantle. *"You call this clean? You are the laziest woman."* She watched as Bill walked over to her and grabbed her by the throat and pulled her to the mantle. *"Look at this filth." Bill took her hair and wiped the mantle with it and then he shoved her, causing Melody to injure her arm.* Instinctively, Melody rubbed her arm remembering how it hurt for a month.

Melody moved onto the dinning room. She looked around the room. Nothing had changed. She saw a crystal vase that had been given to them as a wedding gift. She picked it up and turned it. It revealed the crack that Bill caused when he threw his plate causing it to fall. She was surprised that it didn't break. Melody still thought it was a beautiful vase. Melody placed the vase back down and went on into the next room. She was amazed how well kept the house was. She thought, "He never cleaned or even straightened up when I was living here."

Melody went upstairs. Other than dust from months of neglect everything was in order. As she went to step into her old bedroom Melody felt ill. She stood there for a few minutes to compose herself. Melody stood at the door looking into the room.

As if watching a movie Melody saw her life pass before her: *Bill was standing over her. She had fallen on the floor from him kicking her out of the bed. He was yelling at her because she hadn't asked if she could get pregnant. Melody was laying in bed and began cramping up. She went to get out of bed and felt something going down her leg. It was blood.* Melody watched the terror wash over her face. *She went into the bathroom. She sat on the toilet and a large discharge came out of her. She knew she had lost the baby. When Bill came home Melody informed him. He called her stupid and a sorry excuse for a woman. He told her that she couldn't do anything right. "First you get pregnant without my permission and then I get excited and you are too sorry and weak to carry it. You better not get pregnant again until I tell you." He walked over and slapped her in the head. She cried all night. Bill didn't want to hear it so he went into one of the guess rooms and slammed the door.* Melody continued to watch her life pass by. All the abuse, verbal and physical.

She placed her hands to her face to stop the tears. She didn't want to cry. Melody had shed so many tears because of this man. When Davis walked up from behind her she didn't hear him. He placed his arms around her. He went to kiss her neck and she jumped. Melody turned around. Davis saw that her face was drenched with tears.

"Are you alright?"

"I will be. I can't stay here. Can you take care of this for me."

Davis placed his hand under her chin.

"I'll do whatever you need me to do."

"Thank you."

Melody walked quickly down the hall and down the stairs. She walked outside. Davis followed behind her. The realtor pulled up. Davis introduced the two. Melody informed the realtor that Davis would be handling the sale. She informed her that if there was anything to do with the removal of the items in the house to contact Davis. Melody also told the realtor that she would be willing to add the items in the house to the sale. Melody informed the realtor that most of the items in the house were no more than five years old. The realtor thanked her and then went into the house.

Davis asked, "Are you going to be alright?"

"Yes. It's just there are a lot of bad memories here."

"Would you like some company tonight?"

"I don't want you to stop whatever you were doing."

"Don't worry about it. I'll stop and get something for dinner and get a couple of movies. What would you like to eat?"

"Chinese."

"You want seafood?"

"Yes."

"I'll order a few things and bring them over. What do you want to drink?"

"Soda is fine."

"I'm going to bring you something good."

"Ok, I'll see you soon."

After Melody left she headed home. Her cell phone rang.

"Hello."

"Hi."

"Collin?"

'Yes, who else? Don't answer that. How are you?"

'I'm okay."

"Are you sure? You sound different."

"I just came from Bill's house. I went in and it brought back all the things that happened there. Too many bad memories. I asked Davis to do what is needed inside."

"I'm sorry I'm not there. Do you want to talk about it?"

"You will be soon. Yes, if you don't mind." Melody told him what happened. Then she stopped talking.

"Are you there?"

"Yes. Let's talk about you. How are things there?"

"Great. The classes are interesting. Maybe next year you can go as an associate."

"I don't think the school would pay for a new employee to take such an important trip."

"You never know. You are very bright."

"I guess."

"Melody I hate to go, but it's late and I have an early morning. I'll see you soon."

"Okay. Be safe."

Melody hung up the phone. She was happy to hear from Collin. She appreciated the distraction. Talking to Collin made her travel home quicker. Melody parked the car and then went inside. Again she felt that lonesome feeling. She thought of how when Collin was there he seemed to fill the emptiness. Melody went up to her room and changed clothes. She then went into Juanita's room. Melody sat on her daughter's bed. She picked up the photo album and looked at the pictures in it. It seemed such a long time ago and the people in the pictures were almost unrecognizable. She thought, "Who are these happy people? Could that be me, smiling, looking like I don't have a care in the world? Look at my little girl. She was so beautiful and my husband, (Melody smiled) how handsome." Melody ran her hand over the picture. She laid down and held the album to her chest. Tears ran down her face. Melody drifted off to sleep...........

An hour went by. Melody awakened to the sound of the doorbell ringing. She laid there a few seconds trying to figure out where she was. When Melody realized where she was and who was probably at the door Melody got up. She smoothed the bed out and left the room.

As Melody walked pass the mirror in the hallway she checked herself. She went to the bathroom and washed her face. Melody combed her hair. She then ran down the hall and down the stairs. She opened the front door.

"Hi. I'm sorry I took so long to open the door."

"Not a problem. Are you okay?"

"Yes. I'm fine. I had fallen asleep."

"Are you hungry? (Davis held up the bags) I brought food."

"I'm sorry, come in." Davis followed Melody into the den. "You can place the food on this table."

"I know you told me that you were fine with soda, but I brought something a little stronger than soda. Here are the movies." Davis handed Melody the bag with movies in it. Melody took the movies out of the bag and placed one of them into the DVD.

"I hope they're okay."

"I wanted to see both of these."

Melody left out of the room to make the drinks. When she returned Davis had made plates for them. Melody came into the room sipping on her drink. She sat down and gave Davis one of the glasses. Davis taste the drink.

"This is good. Where did you learn to make drinks?"

"Juan. Before we had Juanita he used to make different drinks for us. I miss the times that we had together. I'm sorry."

"For what?"

"I know you don't want me to talk about my husband. Let's start the movie."

Melody said grace and they began to eat. The movie began to play. Davis moved onto the love seat pretending he couldn't see the movie as well from the angle he was sitting. They sat side by side eating and watching the movie. A couple of times Melody screamed and Davis laughed.................

After they were finished eating Melody went to the wet bar and brought in a pitcher that was filled with green snaps. They sipped the liquor. Melody leaned back into Davis' arms. He placed his arm around her shoulder. They were half way finished the liquid when Melody put in the second movie. Davis and Melody watched the movie and continued to sip on their drinks................

When the movie was over Melody decided to put in a comedy. Davis teased.

"What you afraid to go to sleep thinking about the movie?"

"I just don't like to sleep on a scary movie."

Melody left out of the room. She made another pitcher of green snaps. Melody returned to the den and filled Davis' glass. She took a sip of hers and sat down. She laid her head on his shoulder. Davis placed his arm around her shoulders. They laughed at the show that they were watching. Davis caressed her shoulder. Melody did not protest. She continued to watch the show. Davis took his free hand and put it up to Melody's chin. He turned her face towards his. He leaned in looking into her eyes. When she didn't protest he lightly kissed her lips. He looked into her eyes again. He then kissed her again. This time he lingered. Melody responded by placing her hand on his arm. She could feel his muscles through his shirt. Davis teased her lips with his tongue. They continued to kiss. Davis pulled her into him and caressed her back. Melody squeezed his arm. Davis knew she was turned on at his point. Davis adjusted his body where Melody leaned back leaving him to lean over her. He caressed her body and kissed her all over. Their passion rose leaving only one thing left to do. As they made love Melody thought of how skillful Davis was. Her mind wondered to Collin. Davis could tell the change. He stopped what he was doing. Davis whispered, "Are you alright?"

"Yes."

Davis kissed her with such passion that Melody no longer thought of anything, but how Davis was making her feel.....................

The next morning Davis awakened at ten. He smiled down at Melody as she slept. He eased himself off of her and found the bathroom. He took a quick shower and then dressed. Davis saw that there was a pad and paper on the table in the hallway.

He wrote: ***"Gorgeous thanks for a memorable night. I got the movies and will return them. I will call you later in the week. Talk to you soon."***

Davis

Second Chances

Chapter 11

Melody awakened a half hour later. She looked around and saw that she was in the den. Melody looked down and saw that she was naked. She remembered her night. Melody got up. As she was walking towards the stairs Melody noticed the note. As she walked up the stairs Melody read it. She felt better that Davis had not just left. She went into her bathroom and turned on the shower. Melody stepped into the shower and began to soap up her body. As she did so Melody remembered Davis' touch. She thought of how skillful he was. Melody remembered how strong his hands were, but also how smooth and gentle. She remembered how his lips burnt everywhere he placed them. Melody was getting aroused just thinking about it. Melody rinsed the soap off of her. She dried off and put on a bath robe. She was still tired. She laid down and drifted off to sleep.

Several hours later she was awakened by her cell phone.

"Hello."

"Hi gorgeous. Did I wake you?"

"Yes. That's okay."

"Are you still asleep? Rough night?"

"Don't be funny."

"Are you up for company?"

"Sure."

"Great. I'll pick up something for dinner and bring it over. How's an hour from now?"

Melody looked at the clock. It was four o'clock. She couldn't believe that she had slept all day and to think of it hadn't eaten.

"That sounds fine. I'll see you at five."

"Okay, see you soon gorgeous."

Melody hung up the phone. She got up and looked in her closet. She selected some jeans and a button down sweater.

By five Melody was dressed and had gone downstairs.

When the doorbell rang she answered it right away. Davis smiled and leaned over to kiss Melody.

"Come in."

"You look beautiful."

"Thank you."

They sat down. Davis took the plates out the bag. He began fixing their plates. When Davis was finished he took two ice teas from another bag.

"You do drink ice tea right?" Melody looked at him suspiciously. "They're virgin."

Melody took hers and drank out of it. "This is good. Thank you."

They began to eat. As the two ate Davis told her that he had to leave early to take care of some matters with Bill's house. Davis explained that he had the house aired out and was having them dust the place. Davis told her that she could expect to get a good price for the house, since it was in excellent condition and in a prime location.

When they were finished eating Davis asked if Melody wanted to go for a walk. She agreed. They walked hand in hand for several blocks.

When they returned to her house Davis told Melody that he couldn't see her for a few days, that he had a few things to work on Monday. He kissed her and then left.

Melody cleaned the den. She put the leftovers in the kitchen. Melody cleaned the den. She put the left over food in the refrigerator. Melody took her ice tea up to her room. She sat in her chase and leaned back. Melody closed her eyes. Immediately Collin came to mind. She wondered what he was doing. Melody thought of how she missed him.

Melody thought of the four men that she had been with. Bill had been her first. He had been experienced and knew what a woman liked. While in bed he was attentive and gentle, but when they were awake he was very different. With him she followed his lead and never could imagine the things that she had done with these other three men.

She guess Juan was the one who broke Melody out of her shell. He had been so kind and gentle with her. Juan had actually encouraged Melody to let go of her inhibitions. Many times she had cried after they had made love. Melody had never imagined that a relationship could be as wonderful as she had with Juan. Juan had been all the things that Bill wasn't. Juan had shown her patience and taught Melody to love herself. He made her believe that she deserved to be happy and treated with kindness. Melody thought of these two new men in her life.

Collin had started out as a friend. Someone who she could go to and confide in. Because he was her mentor Melody felt comfortable with him. He was very patient with her. Collin's ways reminded her of Juan. Many of their ways were similar. She did notice that his love making was different. Both Collin and Davis were more skillful lovers. They were more adventuress as well. Melody noticed while both men were excellent lovers Collin and Davis touch were different.

She thought about Davis. He was nice and he was always attentive when they were together. Davis was more forward and assure of himself. He was similar to Juan when it came to his forwardness. Melody fell asleep thinking of these men...............................

As the weeks went by Melody finished school. She was set to graduate the week that Collin was scheduled to return. Her parents were proud of her and excited about the graduation. They planned a party for her. Her mother asked Melody if there was anyone she wanted to invite. Melody had a dilemma. She would like both Collin and Davis to share in her happiness. But since her relationship had evolved with both men from just friends to something more, with sleeping with them both, Melody knew since this had happened both men would expect her to act the part....

Two days before Melody's graduation Collin called and informed her that he was remaining in Europe an extended period. Melody's heart dropped. Collin told her that he had given his recommendation to keep her on and wished her well. Melody shield her disappointment and thanked him. When she got off the phone Melody thought of their weekend together. "Had it been just casual sex? He always said that they were friends." Melody called Davis. His secretary answered the phone, with an irritated voice she told Melody to hold on. Davis picked up the phone.

"Davis."

"Hi."

"Melody?"

"Yes."

"Sarah didn't say it was you. She just said a client was on the phone. I'm glad to hear from you. I just got word from Joyce the realtor. She said that she has a buyer. They bargained that you pay closing and I told them that would be fine. It'll come out of the sale. Is that to your approval?" Melody was impressed. She found Davis charming in his work façade.

"That's fine. Just let me know when to come in for the closing."

"Will do. Now that is out of the way, what do I deserve the pleasure of this phone call?"

"I graduate on Friday. My parents are throwing a party and I was wondering if you would like to come."

"I am actually free on Friday. What time is your graduation?"

"Eleven in the morning."

"I'll be there."

"You sure I'm not taking you away from anything?"

"No. I don't have any meetings. I'll cut out early. Is the get together right after?"

"We plan to go out to eat and then I'm going home to change and go over later, about six."

"Okay. I'll come to the graduation, then return to work and come by after work. I'll meet you at your parent's about seven. Is that alright?"

"That's fine." Melody gave Davis all of the information.

"I'll see you Friday. Congratulations Gorgeous."

It was something special in his voice when he called her that. It wasn't as if he was coming on to her or even trying to make her feel good. It was like a pet name that was only meant for her and it had something she couldn't explain the way it made her feel.

"Ok."

Melody hung up the phone. Melody called her mother and informed her that she had invited Davis. Her mother was happy that she was getting out and was not holding onto the past.........................

Thursday was very busy for Melody. By the time Melody returned home she was exhausted. Melody laid across the bed with her clothes on. She drifted off to sleep. Melody began to dream:

Melody walked into her mother's house. Everyone yelled congratulations. Each person walked up to her and hugged her. Off in the distance was Juan. Although he was off in the distance she could tell it was him. As the guest hugged Melody her focus was on Juan. She wanted so much for him to come closer. After everyone had said their good wishes Melody began walking towards Juan. He did not move. As she got closer Juan held out his arms. Melody went into them. "You're really here. I miss you so much."

He whispered, "I miss you too. I'm proud of you. Baby you have to let me go. There's a good man waiting for you to give yourself to him. He wants to give you all of him, but he's afraid that you won't because you're holding onto me. What we had was wonderful, but it's in the past. You have to let go of us. You have a new life waiting for you and you are going to miss it if you don't let me go."

"I love you so much. We were so happy. I don't know how to let you go."

"Remember me and Juanita, but stop grieving us. You need your love for your new family." Juan kissed her. As she tried to hold on he began to disappear. The last thing she heard was, "Be happy."

Melody woke up. She looked at the clock. It was five o'clock in the morning. The sun had come up. Melody laid there thinking of her dream. She wondered who was this new man and was she really going to have a new family?

A half hour later her phone rang. She reached over and answered it.

"Hello."

"Hi. I hope I didn't wake you."

"No, I was just laying here."

"How do you feel?"

"Alright."

"Just alright? Woman you should be very proud of your accomplishment. I'm sorry that I couldn't be there."

"That's alright. You had a life before and you have to be there."

"I'm your friend. I wanted to be there for you."

"You called. You didn't have to. So I appreciate that."

"Is Davis going to be there?"

Melody thought about the question. She was surprised at Collin asking about Davis.

Reluctantly she answered, "Yes."

"Well I'm happy someone is there with you. I have to go now. Enjoy yourself. You have a lot to be proud of. You are a survivor. I hope to see you soon."

"Thank you for calling. I'll see you when you get back. Be safe."

They got off the phone. Melody laid back down. She wondered which man or if it was even Davis or Collin that Juan was referring to. Melody forced herself to get up. She went into the bathroom and took a shower. Melody took the dress that she had purchased for the graduation out. She put lotion over her body and sprayed matching perfume over it. She placed her stockings on and then her dress. Melody picked her gown up on the way out the door.

When she stepped out of her house Davis was there in his Bentley. He got out and walked up to her. He kissed her lightly on the lips. He put his arm out and she placed her arm in his. They walked to his car. Davis opened the passenger side door. Melody got in. Davis closed the door behind her and then walked over to the driver side. He got into the car. Before pulling off he said, "You look beautiful."

"Thank you. What are you doing here? I thought that you would show up at the graduation."

"You should have an escort for such an important day."

"Thank you."

"No need. This is a big day for you. I remember when I graduated from law school. My parents were so excited. They threw this huge party. I appreciated it, but I was young and wanted to do my own thing."

"Did you go?"

"Of course. They paid for my education. I stayed a few hours and then made my get away."

"So you had a great night."

"Yes. It wasn't so bad with my parents. You know I was impressed that you invited me."

"I'm happy you accepted."

Davis and Melody made light conversation for the rest of the ride.....................

When they arrived at the school Davis left Melody off in front of the school. He told her that he'd catch up with her after the graduation. He lightly kissed her on the lips.

Melody walked into the school. She put on her cap and gown. Melody got in line and the group began to walk to their seats. As she sat and listened to the speeches Melody thought of her life up until now. A good feeling came over her. Melody realized that God was giving her a second chance at her dreams. She had always wanted to go to college and now she was at her graduation, receiving her doctorates. Melody's name was called. She stood and began walking towards the stage. Her parents and Davis stood up. They were clapping. Melody smiled. When she got to the stage Melody was given her certificate. She paused a moment. Melody's father took her picture. Melody walked off the stage.

After the graduation was over, Melody met up with Davis and her parents.

Soon after Davis found his way to them. Melody introduced Davis to her parents. They invited him to go to lunch with them, but he declined, explaining that he had to return to work. He told her parents that he would be at the party. During their meal Melody's mother drilled her about Davis. Melody told her mother of his profession and that he was helping her sale Bill's place. Melody told her parents how she met Davis. Her mother probed further, asking about Melody's feelings towards this man. Melody hesitated and then said that she thought Davis was charming. Melody didn't go any further. She changed the subject. Her mother offered Melody their home to come back to. Melody assured her parents that she was dealing with her lost. She thanked her mother for the offer.

After they had talked for an hour the family got up and left the restaurant. Melody's parents gave her a ride home.

When they pulled up in front of her house Melody stayed in the car for a few minutes looking at her house. She stared thinking of her life there. Melody recalled the first time that she came to this house. It wasn't a good time in her life. Then she thought of the day she came to stay and all of the wonderful memories that came after. She then thought of how this was the first time that she was on her own. Melody thought of her dream. She wondered which guy was Juan referring to when he told her there was another man or was it either guy. Melody's mind then thought of the family Juan spoke of. She placed her hand on her stomach and thought, "Could it really be true, I'm going to have more children?" She felt excited thinking of it. Melody's cell phone rang. She quickly answered it.

"Hello."

"Hi. I'm running a little late, but I'm still coming."

"Okay. That's fine."

"Where are you? I tried calling your house."

"Oh. I am outside. I was just about to go in."

"Well I'm not going to keep you. I just didn't want you to think that I wasn't coming."

"Thanks for calling."

"I'll see you later."

"Okay."

The two hung up the phone. Melody got out of her car said bye to her parents and went into her house. Melody took her clothes off and laid down. She drifted off to sleep. She slept for a couple of hours.

When she awakened Melody got up and freshened up. She put on the outfit she purchased for the party. Melody sprayed perfume over herself. She got her car keys and then left the house. Melody got in the car and drove off.

A half hour later Melody arrived at her mother's. Melody pulled into the driveway and then got out of the car. Melody rang the doorbell and then went into the house. As she entered Melody's mother met her and they hugged. Each guest greeted her. They congratulated and hugged Melody. Melody mingled with her cousins and friends. The guest made a few toast to Melody.

By the time Davis arrived Melody had had a few drinks and was feeling good. When Davis walked up to her, Melody was smiling ear to ear. He gave her a light kiss on the lips.

Melody said, "Thanks for coming."

Music was playing. Melody took Davis by the hand and led him to the living room where others were dancing. They began to dance.

After a few songs Melody asked Davis if he would like a drink. Davis declined stating that he would be the designated driver. The party went on until three in the morning. Melody's mother asked her if she wanted to stay the night. Melody told her that she was going home. Davis assured Melody's mother that he would get her home safely. Melody left her car at her parent's. Davis drove her home. When they arrived at Melody's house she asked him in. Davis accepted the invitation. Melody fixed them a drink and then turned some music on. She sat next to Davis.

"Did you enjoy yourself?"

"It was nice. Well we know you enjoyed yourself."

"I did. I haven't enjoyed myself with my family in a long time. Before Bill. Let's not talk about that. I love this song. Dance with me?"

Davis got up. He held his hand out. Melody took it. He pulled her into his arms. They swayed to the music.

"You seem different."

"Do I? I feel different. I feel free."

Davis spin Melody around and then pulled her back into his arms. Melody laid her head on his chest. As the music played on Melody and Davis continued to dance. Davis placed one of his hands behind Melody's neck. She looked up at him. Davis leaned in. Melody moved close and closed her eyes. Davis lightly kissed her. He sampled her lips. "Hmmh the drink taste better from your lips."

They began to kiss. Davis picked Melody up and carried her to the couch. He gently laid her down. Davis took his suit jacket off. He looked down at Melody.

"You are so beautiful."

Davis bent down and kissed Melody on the lips. He kissed her chest. He took the back of his hand and smoothed it down her chest. Davis caressed her body. Melody didn't move. She laid still enjoying how Davis was making her feel. Melody didn't want this feeling to end. Melody looked at Davis through eyes of passion. Davis seemed to be in a trance, turned on by the way her body was responding under his touch.

Although Melody wanted to reach out and pull Davis to her she lay patient. Davis stopped for a second and took off his shirt, exposing his muscular chest. Melody couldn't' resist. She caressed it. Davis removed her blouse exposing her lace bra. This seemed to further arouse Davis. He bent down and kissed her. While they kissed Davis laid next to Melody. He caressed her breast. He smoothed his hand down the flat of her stomach. He moved down and kissed her stomach. Melody loved the way that Davis was making her feel. Her body screamed for him to complete it, but Davis did not obliged. He continued to drive her senses to madness. Melody reached out and loosened his belt. He stopped what he was doing and allowed her to undress him. When he was naked Melody laid back. Davis took his time removing the rest of her clothes. His hands were so strong. They were smooth and gentle. She shifted her body not able to remain still any longer. She wrapped her arms around his neck. Davis kissed her with controlled passion. After what seemed to be an eternity Davis granted Melody her wish. Davis held her to him. She held his shoulders. Her body was so turned on it was maddening. Davis was so controlled that their love making went on for hours. They were both drenched in sweat. It was sweet and dripped off of them as if to cool down their bodies. Melody had never felt so much pleasure. As Davis finally allowed his body to sub-come to it's pleasure he pulled her closer. Melody again held onto Davis taking in his pleasure.

They both collapsed. The two layed holding onto each other, not speaking afraid that the moment would disappear. Davis caressed her body sending shivers throughout it. He kissed her lips tasting the sweat from their passion. Soon he laid his head on her chest and the two drifted off to sleep...

When they awakened Melody and Davis were still in each other's arms. He kissed her. Melody thought about how he made her feel. Laying in his arms she thought how nice it felt, but it was different. Davis was very skilled and caring. Melody asked herself, "Could he be the man Juan spoke of?"

"Hey, what are you thinking about?"

"Nothing. Are you hungry? I can fix something."

"Let me take you out to eat."

"I have to get dressed."

"While you get dressed I'll go home and change clothes."

"Are you sure?"

"Yes. I won't be long."

He kissed her again and then got up. He picked up his clothes and went into the bathroom. When he came out Davis was dressed. Davis left out the door, got into his car and headed home. Melody picked up her clothes and then went upstairs. She went into the bathroom and turned on the shower. Just as she went to step into the shower her telephone began to ring. She ran to answer it.

"Hello."

"Hi Gorgeous."

"Hi."

"It's Collin."

"I know who it is." (She lied)

"How was the graduation?"

"It was nice. How are things there?"

"Kind of lonely."

"There aren't any women there?"

"I'm not interested in meeting any women over here."

Melody smiled to herself.

"So when are you coming back?"

"They want me to stay a while longer. They are building a therapy center here and want me to interview prospective employees."

Collin described the facility. He went on to tell her everything that he had been doing in Europe.

"Wow, that sounds great."

"So how is it going?"

"It's going. Things are moving along."

"Melody I miss talking to you."

"I miss you too. I mean I miss talking to you too."

"Really?" Collin's heart leaped.

"Yes."

It was quiet for a few minutes.

"Well Melody I better go. I'll call you soon. Take care."

"You too."

When Collin hung up he thought about Melody's statement, how she had said that she missed him. He wanted to tell her that he missed her too, that he missed everything about her. He thought about their weekend together. Collin hoped that Melody would still be single and that she would be interested in a relationship with him when he got back.

After Melody hung up the phone she realized how much she missed Collin. She wondered if Collin would come back. Melody thought of what Juan had told her. She wondered, "If it was Collin, wouldn't he come back? Maybe I should ask him, but what if all we have is friendship? But what about that night? Was it just a fling. Was it that he had too much to drink?" Melody realized that she was in love with Collin. "What can I do?"

Melody went into the shower. She realized that it was late and Davis would be coming back soon. She showered quickly. Melody came out of the shower and grabbed some jeans and a fitted sweater. She heard the doorbell. Melody ran downstairs and opened the door. She turned and as she ran back up the stairs Melody yelled, "I'm sorry, I have to comb my hair and put on my shoes. I'll be right down."

"Don't worry, I have time."

When Melody came back down she went into the living room where Davis was seated. He was looking at the pictures on the mantle.

"I've been meaning to put those away."

"Are you ready?"

"I have to move on."

Davis got up and walked over to her.

"Are you ready for a serious relationship?"

Melody knew that he meant with him.

"I am." She meant with Collin.

Davis held her arms and bent to kiss her. Melody liked Davis. She hated leading him on. She was attracted to him, but not in love. She didn't want to be alone and what if Collin never came back? Melody thought, "Maybe Davis is the man. Maybe you only get one love." Then she thought, "I love another. Why would I fall in love with a man who doesn't love me, but then again I once loved Bill and what did that get me? Juan told me that I had a chance and not to blow it."

"Are you ready?"

"Yes."

Melody got her coat and they left. As they drove Davis placed his hand on Melody's leg. She noticed the difference in his behavior. She could sense that he considered them to be a couple. Davis talked about his job. He then mentioned that he had gotten word about Bill's house and they had two prospective buyers. He told her the offer. Melody was impressed and told him she was willing to accept either offer. Davis told her that he would pass that along to the realtor.

When they arrived at the restaurant they were quickly seated. Davis made light conversation. Melody pondered over her feelings. She thought maybe she could learn to love Davis. Davis realized that Melody's mind was not with him.

"Are you okay?"

"I'm sorry. I have a few things on my mind. I'm not good company."

The waitress came over and interrupted their conversation. She took their order and then left.

"I understand. After we eat would you like me to take you by your parents to get your car?"

"Would you? I do appreciate all of your help."

"It's my pleasure."

The waitress returned with their food. She placed it down on the table. Melody and Davis began to eat. Davis looked at Melody like a man in love. She tried not to look at him. All Melody could feel was guilt.

When they were finished eating Davis and Melody left the restaurant. Davis drove Melody to her parent's house. Melody thanked Davis. He kissed Melody and told her that he'd call her in a week....

Two weeks later Melody was offered a position at the school. She accepted it. She hadn't heard from Collin. Melody wondered if he thought of her and if he would ever come back. Melody told Davis of the position and he offered to take her out to celebrate. Melody told him that she wasn't up for celebrating. She told him that things were happening so fast that she hadn't had time to breathe. Melody told him that she needed time. Davis accepted the excuse and told her that he would give her a call soon……….. The next day Melody received flowers from Davis. She called his cell phone when she thought he would be unable to answer it. Melody left a message saying, "Thank you so much for being such a wonderful guy and thank you for the beautiful flowers and card."

Melody hung up the phone.

A month went by and Melody had not spoken to either Davis or Collin. Although she missed them in their own way, Melody was happy to have the space to think. She was happy to be working. Melody was getting comfortable in her new job. She enjoyed what she was doing. Melody sometimes stayed in her office after everyone left. She didn't want to go home. Something was missing.

Christmas was coming up. Melody's parents insisted on her coming over. Melody was kind of down and really wanted to stay home……………………..

When Christmas finally came Melody got up early. She cleaned the house and then got ready to go to her parents. After dressing Melody left for her parents. Melody was surprised when she arrived at her parents and the house was full with Melody's relatives. Everyone was singing and enjoying the day. Melody found herself joining in and enjoyed herself……………………….

As it got late Melody thanked her parents for inviting her and making her day happier than she expected it to be. Her parents hugged Melody and told her that they love her.

When Melody returned home her cell phone went off. She looked down at it. It was Collin. She answered it right away. When he spoke his voice made her miss him even more. Melody longed for his touch. Melody thought she heard something in Collin's voice, but dismissed it. They didn't talk of anything important. Collin asked how she had been. Melody followed suit. Although very little was said Melody felt as if Collin wanted to say something, but held back. He only stayed on for a short while and then told her that he had to go. He wished her a Merry Christmas and then hung up.

Soon after she hung up with Collin Davis called and informed her that there would be a closing on Bill's house on December twenty-seventh. Melody was thrilled to finally be getting rid of the house and further move on with her life...................

Melody decided to show up at the closing. She wanted to see the house, for her to finally be done with her past life. When Melody showed up at Davis' office she was escorted into his office. Davis got up and hugged her. Melody felt a familiar feeling and then he released her. Melody looked at him. She saw longing in his eyes. When the secretary came into his office and announced that the couple who were purchasing the house had arrived his look changed to business.

Davis instructed his secretary to come in and their attorney followed them…………………………....

After the closing Davis asked Melody if she wanted to go out to celebrate. She accepted. They went out to dinner and then a club. Davis and Melody danced to several songs. There were occasions where Melody was enjoying Davis company and then she would think of Collin. She remembered their going out dancing. When Davis touched her she longed for it to be Collin. They left the nightclub after it closed.

After they left the club Davis took Melody home. They sat in his car. Davis took his hand and cupped Melody's face.

"Beautiful what happened?"

Melody looked down.

"I don't know. I think I moved too fast and wasn't ready for us. You are a wonderful man, but I don't think we were meant to be. I appreciate all that you have done for me. I don't want to lead you on. Anyway I think I need to be by myself to find out who I am. You know this is the very first time that I've been on my own. In a strange way it feels good."

"Well if you ever want to go out call me and if you decide you want to go out for New Years Eve give me a call. I'll be checking on you." Davis leaned over and kissed Melody. "I'm going to miss you."

"Me too."

"Take care of yourself beautiful."

"You too."

Melody got out of the car. She walked up to her door. After opening the door Melody turned around. She blew a kiss at Davis and then waved. Melody went into the house and closed the door behind herself. Melody leaned back onto the door and closed her eyes for a few minutes. The warmth of Davis kiss was still on her lips. She could still smell the scent of his cologne on her from their dancing together. Melody opened her eyes and then went upstairs. She removed her clothes and went into the shower. As the warm water rain over her body Melody thought of Davis. Melody wondered if she had made a mistake. After washing her body Melody dried off and got into bed. Melody laid in bed and thought about her life. She spoke out loud as if talking to Juan.

"Juan did I make the right choice? Did I screw up my second chance? Look I'm living alone and I'm doing okay. I still miss you and my beautiful baby girl. Give her a kiss for me." Melody said a prayer and then drifted off to sleep....

New Years Eve Melody called Davis and wished him a blessed New Year. She went over to her parent's home and brought in the New Year with them. They invited some friends and family over. Melody had a good time and decided to spend the night. She slept in her old room.

As she laid in her childhood bed Melody thought of her life. She thought of her girlfriends, how she had so much fun and thought of how her life would be. She tried to remember her childhood plans. She laughed thinking of wanting to be a dancer. Melody thought of the kind of husband she would marry. She sighed thinking of how she was so young when she met Bill and somehow he had made her believe that he was the man that she was suppose to end up with. Her dreams were no longer her own and how she had taken on the roll of being the perfect woman for him.

Melody then thought of Juan, how he had been her night in shining armor. How he had come out of nowhere and captured her heart. Juan had brought her closer to her family and returning her to what she had thought a husband, a family should be.

Then Collin came to mind. She smiled, thinking of how he was so warm and understanding. He warmed her heart whenever she talked to him or he was around. He was her best friend and made her feel better than anyone ever had.

For a brief moment Melody thought of Davis. She also smiled thinking of him. He was perfect. Perfect for someone who liked the superficial life. He was genuine, but he was very business and matter of fact. Melody thought of how she could see why he and Bill were friends. Not that she thought Davis would be abusive, but they wanted the perfect woman. She didn't want to be that perfect woman anymore. She didn't want to feel that she had to try so hard. Collin made her feel comfortable and knew he thought she was perfect no matter what. Melody soon drifted off to sleep...........................

The next day she had breakfast with her parents. When she got ready to leave her parents asked if she was sure she wanted to leave. Melody kissed them both and told them that she had a wonderful time and was happy that they had become a family again. Melody assured them that she was happy with her life and that they didn't have to worry about her.

When she got home Melody cleaned out her house. She put away pictures of her old life. She packed away all of Juanita's things. Melody called the veterans and donated all of Juan's and Juanita's clothes. She donated Juanita's toys as well. Melody took a week off work and painted over Juanita's room. She removed the curtains and bed covering. When Melody was done, her house showed no sign of her past life. Like the New Year she was starting a new life, out with the old and in with the new...........................

As time passed Melody enjoyed her new house. She made friends at work and occasionally had small get togethers with them. Melody occasionally felt a longing when walking, pass Collin's office. It no longer made her sad. She was happy for her time with him. He and Davis had taught her, that she could feel passion and Bill had no power over her. She was a survivor. Although she had men who were interested in her, Melody had turned them down. Melody had grown into a strong woman. She sometimes smiled at the thought of it.

On Melody's thirtieth birthday she went out with some friends. She happened to run into Davis. He hugged her. One of her friends divulged that it was Melody's birthday. Davis asked her for a dance. They danced to two songs. As they danced Davis asked how she was doing. He told her that he missed her and sometimes thought of calling her. Davis remembered that he had brought a woman to the club. He took Melody's face in his hands and kissed her on the side of her face. "You look beautiful as always. I hope you get all the wishes that you deserve. Happy Birthday."

He walked Melody back to her friends. Melody watched as Davis walked over to his guest. The woman wrapped her arm around his arm. For a brief moment Melody felt a tinge of jealously. Melody couldn't help wondering if she had made the right decision. One of the women that was with her said, "Girl he is fine."

"Yes he is. He's just a friend."

"I wish I had friends that gorgeous. You should make him more than a friend."

"Nah. He's where he should be."

"I couldn't imagine letting that go."

"Well Lisa sometimes you have to think of others."

"I guess."

"This is my favorite song."

Melody and Lisa went onto the dance floor. The DJ said, "This goes out to Melody, Happy Birthday."

Melody looked at Lisa.

"Wasn't me."

Melody looked over and saw Davis holding a drink up as if he was toasting to her. She smiled and nodded her head to thank him. Melody continued to dance. A man came over and began to dance with them. They danced to a few songs and then Melody went to sit down. Lisa stayed on the dance floor. A couple of guys walked over to Melody and asked her to dance, but she turned them down. Before Davis left with his friend Melody noticed him staring at her a few times. Melody told the other women that had come with them that she was tired and was going home....

Second Chances

Chapter 12

Three months had gone by. Melody had settled into her new life. She got up and dressed as usual. Melody fixed herself a light breakfast and then went to work. Melody went into her office. She looked over some papers. She had one client scheduled at ten. After her session Melody went on line and went on her bank site. Melody realized that she had yet to make a donation using the money that she received from the sale of Bills' house. She went into her purse and wrote out two checks, one for battered women's shelter and the other for the agency that counsels men who batter. Melody placed the checks in envelopes and then stepped out of her office to mail them. As she walked to the mailbox she noticed the door to Collin's office was cracked. Melody cautiously walked towards the door. She wondered if someone had taken his job. Melody slowly pushed the door open. To her amazement Collin was seated at his desk. Melody just stood there astonished. Collin hadn't heard her come in. She stood there waiting for him to notice her.

When Collin looked up and saw Melody he smiled. It warmed her heart. He got up and walked over to her. He took her into his arms and hugged her. He pulled back. He cupped her face and then kissed her passionately. Melody placed her hands on his arms. Collin realized what he was doing and stopped abruptly. Collin placed his hands on the side of Melody's face.

"I'm sorry. I missed you."

Melody could see how happy he was.

"Don't be sorry. I missed you too. What are you doing here? I haven't heard from you in months."

"I'm sorry about that. I didn't call you because I was trying to get finish with my work. I also wanted to give you space. I thought it might confuse you if I kept calling you. I wanted you to be sure that whoever you choose to be with would not be influenced by me. If you chose me I wanted you to not have any doubts. How are things with that Davis guy?"

Melody smiled. She saw jealousy.

"He's a good friend."

"Is that it?"

"I went out with him a few times, like you said, but I decided that while he is really a good guy, he wasn't my guy."

"Didn't he like you a lot?"

"Yes. I explained to him that he had a lot to offer, but I didn't feel the same way he did."

"Is it that you weren't ready for a relationship?"

"I was ready. I am ready. I worked out my fears and I let go of my past. I am not the scared little girl that you left."

Collin moved his hands to the back of her neck. Her hair nestled between his fingers. He looked at her. He saw a more mature, self assured woman.

"May I?" Collin drew Melody head closer. He bent closer. Melody lifted her face towards his. Melody closed her eyes. Collin kissed Melody's lips. She allowed him to sample her lips. He kissed her longer. Melody returned his kiss. She wrapped her arms around him. She was so happy that Collin was home and that he seemed to miss her. She had waited so long for this moment. Melody thought maybe for just this moment I'll embrace it. Collin lost control for a brief second; he pulled her closer to his body and then he gained his composure. "Forgive me." Collin moved back. Melody looked confused. "I thought that I would have more control when I saw you again. I guess you being single. You are single?" Melody shook her head yes. "I don't want you to think that I just want to sleep with you." (Melody thought to herself, "That's all I want right now."

"So what do you want?"

"I want a relationship with you."

"We have one."

"What are you saying?"

"Collin I missed you. I stopped Davis from pursuing me."

"Do you think that was wise?"

Melody smoothed her hand down the side of Collin's face.

"All I could think of was you. I evaluated my relationship with him and I thought of what we had. I realized that we had more than just that one weekend. I feel a connection with you. I didn't know what we had at first because you always described us as friends. Then we made love and I evaluated what happened. I never felt that it was casual. I wanted more, but you asked me to figure things out and then I thought maybe it was casual for you. After I stopped hearing from you I did what you said. I went out with Davis, but I kept finding myself comparing what I had and felt with you."

Collin took Melody into his arms. Collin quickly released Melody when he heard a knock on the door.

"Come in."

A student walked into the office.

"Oh I'm sorry. I didn't know you had anyone in here. Professor Salaam said that you were back. I wanted to welcome you back."

"Thank you Jane."

Melody interrupted.

"Well I'll let you get settled in. Welcome back."

The other woman didn't try to stop Melody. Collin touched Melody's arm. "I'll talk to you later."

Melody lightly touched his hand and then left his office. She walked to her office. When Melody went into her office and closed the door she thought of what had just happened.

"Could it be true? Collin is back and he is still attracted to me? Is this my second chance?"

Throughout Melody's work day she was in good spirits. She tried to maintain her composure, but it was difficult. She was excited at the thought of how Collin had responded when he saw her. She could still feel the strength of his touch and the warmth of his lips. Melody didn't see Collin the rest of the day..........................

When the work day was over Melody decided not to go towards Collin's office. She went to her car and drove home............................

When Melody arrived home she parked her car. She went inside her house, placed her purse down and then went into the kitchen. She got a few things out of the refrigerator and fixed a small meal. As Melody sat eating she looked at the small plate and meal. She thought of how nice it would be to cook for a husband and children.

Melody cleaned up the kitchen and then went to bed. She slept soundly basking in the knowledge that Collin had returned...........................

Each day Melody awakened and got ready for work. She avoided walking towards Collin's office. She didn't' want to seem like she was being pushy. Melody was just thrilled that he was back...................................

At the end of the week Melody went home. As usual Melody prepared a small meal for herself and ate. She cleaned up the kitchen, but instead of going up to her bedroom Melody went into her den. She turned the television on and put a DVD into the player. Just as Melody sat back and turned the movie on her telephone rang. Melody reached over the sofa.

"Hello."

"Hi Gorgeous."

"Collin?"

"Yes it's Collin. Sorry I haven't called before now. I was trying to get myself together so I don't screw things up with us."

"Us?"

"Look it's been a long week. Would you like to go out?"

"Tonight?"

"Yes. Would you like to go out dancing?"

"I haven't been in a while."

"Are you busy?"

"No."

"So lets go. How about I pick you up in an hour?"

"I can do an hour."

"Are you sure?"

"I haven't had a good time in a long time. I'll see you in an hour."

"Ok."

Melody turned the television off and then went upstairs. Melody looked into her closet. She had purchased a black dress a year ago and had not worn it. She steamed it and then pulled out a pair of stockings. Melody jumped in the shower. When she came out Melody put lotion on her body and then sprayed cologne over herself. Melody put on her clothes and then curled her hair. She started downstairs just as the doorbell rang. Melody opened the door. Collin reached in and kissed her lightly on the lips.

"Hi. You are beautiful. Are you ready?"

"Yes."

Melody grabbed her purse and then closed the door behind herself. Melody got into Collin's car.

"You look beautiful. I missed you. So tell me what's been happening in your life?"

Melody told Collin everything that had happened to her while he was gone.............. By the time they had arrived at the club Melody had finished her update. Collin parked the car. He and Melody got out of the car. As they walked towards the club Collin put his arm around her waist. Melody liked the way his arm felt.

When they got to the door Collin took his arm from around Melody to open the door. She walked in.

"Would you like to get something to drink?"

"Sure."

They walked over to the bar. Melody ordered a drink. They sat at the bar a few minutes. Melody looked around the club enjoying watching the people dance.

"Would you like to dance?"

"Yes."

Collin took Melody's hand and led her onto the dance floor. When they got there the two began to dance. While they were dancing someone came up from behind Melody and tapped her. Melody turned.

"Hey girl."

"Hi Lisa. What are you doing here?"

"Having fun. Who's the hottie? Lisa looked at Collin up and down."

Melody wasn't sure what to say.

"He's a friend."

"Wow. I must be hanging out in the wrong places. Where are you finding these hot men?"

"Lisa."

"I'm just saying. Ok. I'll leave you with this fine man. He better not be another just friend."

Melody turned back to Collin.

"Who's the friend?"

"A friend from work."

"I couldn't help from over hearing your conversation. It was Davis she was referring to right?"

"Lisa and some other women from work brought me here for my birthday and we saw him here."

"I'm sorry I missed your birthday."

"Don't worry about it."

"Getting back to Larry, is there anything there?"

Melody became bold. She moved closer to Collin. She placed her arms around his shoulders and kissed him. Collin placed his arms around her and returned the kiss. Collin realized where they were and he pulled back. "You are going to have us get arrested."

Melody kissed him again.

"Maybe we should leave."

Collin looked into Melody's eyes.

"Are you sure?"

"Collin take me home."

Collin obliged her. They left the club. Melody and Collin walked to his car and got in. Both were quiet throughout the drive............................

When they arrived at Melody's house she got out of the car. She walked up to her door and then turned around. Collin was still in the car watching her. Melody held her hand out. Collin slowly got out of the car. It seemed an eternity. Collin slowly walked up to Melody's house. She continued holding her hand out. Collin finally made it over to her and took it. Melody held his hand as she opened her front door. She remembered how strong they were and how gentle. Melody locked the door behind them. She continued holding Collin's hand. She led him upstairs to her bedroom. Neither spoke a word.

Collin was caught in a trance of seduction. He followed without saying a word. Collin was turned on by Melody's forwardness. When they entered her room she released Collin's hand. She walked over to her stereo and turned on music. Melody walked back over to Collin.

Melody said, "Dance with me."

Collin took Melody into his arms and they began to dance. He placed his hands on her hips guiding and molding her movements to his. As they danced Melody whispered "I missed you."

Collin cupped her face.

"Gorgeous do you know what you're doing to me?"

Seductively Melody asked, "What am I doing?"

"You got this seductive thing going on. You bring me up to your room and have this soft music going on. You looking sexy as you do and your smell is driving me crazy. You know I thought about you a lot while I was away."

"Did you?"

"What you thought I forgot about you? I couldn't possibly do that."

"I didn't know what to think. I thought maybe that night was just something that happened."

Collin kissed Melody. He pulled her closer. Collin smoothed his hand down her neck and then kissed it. Melody stood there while Collin kissed and caressed her neck. Melody remained standing still. Collin took over the seduction. Collin took off his jacket and laid it on the chair. He then unbuttoned his shirt. Melody had forgotten how well sculpt his body was. He turned her down and then unzipped her dress. He didn't take it of. He smoothed his hand down her back. Collin kissed her back and ran his tongue down it. Melody shivered as he did so. "Are you cold?"

"No."

Collin placed his hands inside her dress. He continued to caress her body. Collin kissed her neck and pulled her closer to his body. He stopped long enough to remove her dress. Collin picked Melody up. He kissed her as he walked towards the bed. Collin gently laid Melody on the bed. He bent down and lightly ran his hand down her body. Collin removed his pants and then laid next to her. He laid there next to Melody and as if touching her with his eyes went over her body with them. Melody's body warmed as she watched his eyes. After what seemed an eternity Collin began kissing her again. It was a long sensual kiss. Melody had long for this moment and wanted it to last forever. Collin caressed Melody's body.

"Your body is burning up."

Melody lightly ran the back of her hand down Collin's face. Collin took her hand and kissed her palm. He then returned to caressing her body. By the time Collin finally answered Melody's call he had touched and caressed every inch of her being. Collin was thorough in his charge of pleasure. Melody held onto his broad shoulders. She kissed his wet body. The couple lost themselves in the rhythmic pleasure..............................

The next morning Collin awakened. Melody was still laying on him. He kissed her forehead. Collin eased her off of him, grabbed his pants and went into the bathroom. He called a restaurant and ordered breakfast. Collin took a quick shower and put on his pants and t-shirt. When he reentered the room Melody was awake. She smiled.

"Good morning. Are you leaving?"

"No, Are you tired of me already?"

"I could never get tired of you."

It warmed his heart the way she looked at him when she made the statement.

"I ordered breakfast. Are you hungry?"

"A little."

Melody got up. As she walked towards the bathroom Collin held his arms out. Melody went into them. He placed his arms around her and caressed her back. Collin kissed Melody on the top of her head. She felt secure in his arms. Melody bask in this feeling.

"Melody I love you. I want to marry you."

Melody looked up into Collin's eyes. Collin got down on one knee. Melody couldn't believe what she was hearing. She had waited so long for someone, now she knew it was Collin to say those words to her.

"Melody I have been in love with you for so long. I gave you your space so you could work things out. You are not the same woman that you were a year ago. You have grown. I can sense that you have made peace with your past. Let me be your future. I want to have a family with you. I want to grow old with you." Collin took her hand. "I don't have a ring right now. I didn't know this was going to happen, but we can go anytime you like to get one. I don't want to waste anymore time. Would you be my wife, my lover, my babies' mother?" (They laughed)

Melody looking in his eyes, smoothed her hand down his face and then kissed him.

"Yes. Yes I'll be your wife."

Collin stood up and took Melody into his arms. He kissed her passionately. He picked her up and carried Melody over to the bed. Their passion turned into a need to be together. Melody had never felt so complete. As Collin made love to her tears filled her eyes. She held onto him never wanting the moment to end.........................

Melody laid in Collin's arms basking in this new remarkable feeling. She listened to his heart beat now steady, after their love making. The doorbell rang. Collin jumped up.

"Oh I forgot the food."

Collin threw on his pants and ran downstairs to take care of the food order. Melody got out of bed and went into the bathroom. By the time Collin came back upstairs Melody had taken a quick shower and put on lounging wear. Collin placed the food down on the coffee table. He went into the bathroom. While he took a quick shower Melody set up the food. When he came out of the bathroom Collin was dressed in only a towel wrapped around him. Melody looked at him. "I'm starved." She gave him a mischievous look.

Collin sat down. He taste the food.

"This is good." Collin fed some to Melody.

"This is good."

Collin and Melody finished eating.

"I have to go home and change clothes."

"Do you have to leave?"

"Yes I have to. I'll tell you what, I'll go home change and then come back. We can go pick out your ring when I come back."

"Are you sure?"

"Melody are you kidding me? I wish I had a ring to give you right now. But this way I can't go wrong because you picked it."

"I'm not really talking about the ring all together. Are you sure you want to get married to me?"

Collin got down on his knees in front of Melody.

"Woman do you know what you do to me? I've been waiting a year for this moment. I want to marry you. Melody answer me something."

"What?"

"Do you love me?"

"Yes."

"Well that's what I wanted to hear. Do you want to take a chance with me?"

"If you want to take a chance with me."

"Why do you say that?"

"I've had two marriages."

"Do you think that weighs any merit on our relationship?"

"I'm sorry. I've put a damper on your proposal."

"No I think it's good to get everything out now. I love you and I want to marry you. I want us to always be together. I want to have babies with you. You are a wonderful woman. You deserve happiness. We deserve to be together. We belong together and we will be very happy together."

"I love you so much. I just want you to be happy."

"That's what I wanted to hear. We've waist over a year where I could have been waking up with you in my arms and you cooking me delicious meals."

Melody smiled. "Yes I will marry you. So when do you want to do this?"

Collin got off his knees, picked Melody up and spin her around.

"Do you want a big wedding?"

"Since this is your first time you choose."

"I just want you. As soon as possible."

"We could have something small. How about September?"

"Let's do it." Collin put on his clothes. He kissed Melody and then left. Melody changed clothes. She cleaned up her room and took the remaining food downstairs. She placed it in the refrigerator. Melody decided to call her mother. She dialed her mother's phone. The phone began to ring.

"Hello."

"Hi mom."

"Hi Baby. How are you?"

"I'm fine. Where's dad?"

"What's wrong?"

"Nothing. I have something to tell you and dad."

Melody's mother called out to her husband. He answered. She told him to pick up the other phone.

"Hello."

"Hi dad."

"Hi sweetheart. How are you?"

"I'm fine dad. I have something to tell you and mom."

"What is it?"

"I'm getting married."

"So you are taken with Davis?"

"No mom. His name is Collin."

"Collin? I thought his name was Davis."

"It's not Davis. I'm getting married to a man name Collin."

"Collin? Have we ever met him?"

"No. He was in Europe when I graduated."

"What happened to Davis? I thought you were dating him."

"I guess I kind of dated him, briefly. He wasn't the one. I've been in love with Collin for a while. When he went to Europe he told me to date. He wanted me to decide who it was I wanted."

"Is he a good guy?"

"Yes dad. He's great."

"Have you picked a day?"

"September. Mom can you help me get things together?"

"Yes. I know a place. It's called Dana's Bread and Breakfast. It has a hall that could hold at least three hundred people."

"We decided to have a small wedding."

"Are you going to have the ceremony in the church?"

"Yes."

"Melody's father said, "Sweetheart congratulations. When are we going to meet this man?"

"I'll try to get him by next weekend."

"You make sure you do. I want to meet this man. I love you."

"I love you too daddy."

Her father got off the phone. Melody and her mother made wedding plans. They hung up an hour later.

Melody's doorbell rang. She answered the door. Collin was dressed in a blue short sleeve shirt and loose fitted jeans. This was the first time she had seen him casual. She thought he looked sexy. Collin kissed Melody lightly on the lips.

"Hi Gorgeous. Are you ready?"

"Yes."

Collin opened the car door for Melody. She got in. He drove off.

"Oh Collin I called my parents and told them that we were getting married. They want to meet you. I told them that I would bring you by next weekend. Is that alright?"

"Why not go today, after we buy your ring?"

"Are you sure?"

"I think that we should. I don't want your parents thinking ill of me because I didn't go to them first."

"I don't think they would hold that against you."

"In any case I would like to meet my future in-laws as soon as possible."

"What about your parents?"

"My mother died when I was eighteen. My father never got over her. He passed ten years later."

"I thought I had heart break. Do you have any sibling?"

"No, I've made peace with it.. I'm an only child."

"So am I."

"Well I don't want that for us. I would like to have more than one child."

"So do I." Melody wrapped her arms around Collin. "I am so excited. I have been having dreams where Juan was telling me that I was going to be blessed with a family and that I would know when that time arise. He also said that I had to let him go or I would loose my chance. I thought that maybe it was Davis at first, but I couldn't stop thinking of you. Things were different with him. I was thrown off by you because you kept saying that we were friends, then you went away and then you told me to see other people. When I saw you that day in your office and you greeted me the way that you did I had hope."

Collin took her hand and squeezed it.

They arrived at the jewelry store. Collin parked. They exited the car and went into the store...........................

After an hour of the couple looking at various rings Melody and Collin finally agreed on an engagement ring and selected wedding bands to match. Collin had their names engraved in the rings. When this was completed the couple left the store and headed to her parent's home. While Collin drove to her parents' home Melody called to tell them that they were coming by...................

When the couple arrived at Melody parent's home Collin parked. They got out of the car and walked up the stairs. Melody rang the doorbell. Her mother opened the door. Melody introduced Collin. Her mother hugged him and said, "Nice to meet you."

Collin was shown to the living room. Melody's mother excused herself and went to get her husband.

When her parents returned Collin was introduced to Melody's father. They shook hands. Melody's mother left the living room again and went into the kitchen. She prepared a light snack for everyone. Melody's mother and father asked Collin about his career, family and personal background. Melody was concerned with them asking so many questions. Melody watched Collin as he calmly answered all of her parent's questions. Melody briefly thought of Bill and how uncomfortable he was with people asking him questions. She remembered when Bill asked for her hand in marriage. Her father was hesitant because of Bill's noticeable irritation to their questions, but because she insisted that they were in love her parents gave their permission.

Looking at Collin now made her love him even more. It brought her comfort, that he never seemed annoyed.

After several hours Melody said that they had to leave. As Melody hugged her mother Mrs. Thomas said, "He's very nice."

Collin kissed Melody's mother and then shook her father's hand.

Collin drove Melody home. He came in for a short while and they talked about the wedding.

When Collin told Melody he had to return home she tried to get him to stay, but he insisted that he needed to leave. Melody accepted his decision. Collin took her by the hand and she walked him to the door. He kissed her lightly on the lips, told her that he loved her and then left.................

After Collin left Melody began straightening her house. As she did so Melody thought of Collin. She smiled thinking of how relaxed he was with her parents. Melody recalled the expression on her father's face when what he called getting to know him, and Melody called drilling Collin. Her father seemed impressed. Melody was happy that her parents seemed pleased with him.

The next few weeks were very busy, with the wedding only being two months away. Melody discontinued taking her birth control pills. She and Collin had agreed that they would begin their family right away. Melody and Collin went to check out Dana's Reception Hall. The couple loved it and booked a space with Dana's daughter...........

Melody and Collin's wedding date had arrived. Melody's mother and Lisa, who she had asked to be her bridesmaid had come over. They helped Melody to get dressed. Although Melody had been married before she decided to wear a white dress anyway. She felt that this was a new life for her and the past had been washed away. After dressing Melody looked into the mirror. She felt like a new person.

Melody walked downstairs and out of the house. The limo was waiting for them. Melody entered the limo first. Lisa entered the limo next and then Melody's mother. The limo pulled off. As they drove to the church Melody thought of her first marriage; how young she was. Melody thought how excited and also how nervous she was. There had been several incidences where Bill had shown aggression. She thought of the wedding and how he stayed close to her, not letting anyone linger around her.

Melody thought of her second wedding. She recalled how attentive Juan was. He was as excited as she was. At the reception they danced most of the night. Juan and Melody had planned to go somewhere special for their tenth anniversary. Melody's mind was jolted back to the present when the limo stopped in front of the church. Melody's mother was escorted into the church first and then Lisa. Melody could hear the music playing. Her father came out of the church. He walked up to Melody. He bent down to kiss her on the cheek.

"You look beautiful."

"Thank you daddy."

Melody's father put his arm out. Melody put her arm in his. They began to walk into the church. When they entered the church everyone stood up. Melody watched Collin's eyes as she walked towards the front of the church. Just as she made it to the front of the church Collin met her. Melody's father placed her arm in Collins'. They walked up to the minister. Melody and Collin recited their vows and then exchanged rings. They were pronounced husband and wife. Collin kissed Melody. Everyone clapped.

Collin and Melody were taken to the reception hall. When they arrived at the hall pictures were taken................................

An hour later Melody and Collin were introduced to their guest.

All during the reception Melody and Collin were as one. Their first dance Collin took Melody into his arms. He held her close. As the music played Collin and Melody were transformed to another world. Though their guest clapped the couple only heard the music and each other's heart beats. After the music stopped the couple remained in each other's arms and continued to dance. The guest began to tap their glasses. A few minutes later the couple's mind returned to their wedding. The couple followed the guest prompts and kissed. Throughout the reception the couple danced and mingled.

At the end of the night Melody and Collin left for their honeymoon................

When they arrived at the airport Collin checked in.

When the airline began boarding Melody and Collin got up. They boarded the plane and quickly found their seats. Collin and Melody talked for most of the flight.

When the plane arrive at their destination Melody became anxious.

After exiting the plane they went to get their bags. A car was waiting for the couple when they exited the airport. They were taken to their hotel.

When they arrived at the hotel, after checking in Collin picked Melody up and carried her into the room. He kissed her and closed the door with his foot. Collin carried her over to the bed. He kissed her passionately. Melody wrapped her arms around Collin's neck.

"I can't believe we're married. I love you so much."

"I love you too."

Melody laid back.

"You know this is the very first time that I've really ever gone anywhere. Juan and I went on a honeymoon, but we didn't come this far."

"You've never been on vacation?"

"Not in the sense of going away. I always thought of it, but I never ventured. Only once. Pretty boring hmm?"

"Not boring, you've just been limited. I promise to take you places. I promise to do all that I can to make you happy."

Melody took Collin's face in her hands and kissed him. No more words were spoken.....

The next day Melody and Collin awakened. They dressed and went out to eat. They toured the island and walked the length of the beach. Throughout their honeymoon the couple took tours every day.

When the end of their trip had come Melody felt sadness. She hated for the trip to end.....

When it came time for them to leave Melody and Collin awakened early. They readied themselves to go to the airport. Melody was quiet as she watched the hotel disappear. When they boarded the plane Melody nestled up to Collin and fell asleep. Melody slept throughout the plane ride. Collin woke her up when they arrived in Newark.

After retrieving their bags the couple walked outside of the airport where a van took them to their car. When they retrieved their car the couple got in and Collin drove them to Melody's house. When they got out of the car Melody and Collin walked up to her front door. Melody opened the door, Collin picked her up and then carried her into the house. Collin kissed Melody and then put her down.

"Are you hungry?"

"I'm starved."

"I'll cook us something."

"Are you sure?"

"Yes. I would like to cook my husband a meal."

"If you insist."

"I do."

Melody prepared a light meal. While she prepared the meal Collin sat and watched her.

"Melody."

"Yes."

"We didn't discuss where we were going to live."

Melody looked at Collin.

"I just thought we would live here."

"Things happened so fast when I got back I didn't have time to think."

"What, you don't want to live here?"

"Melody this is your husband's home."

"Yes, it is."

"No, I mean Juan's home."

"No, it's our home."

"You lived here with him."

"Does it bother you so much?"

"I apologize for not bringing it up sooner. I guess we have a lot to discuss."

Melody fixed their plates and sat them on the table. She sat down. Melody took Collin's hands and closed her eyes. She said a prayer.

"Collin what are you saying?"

"I have my own home and I would like us to live there."

"I've never been to your home."

"Again I apologize."

"Collin don't apologize. I just presumed that we would stay here. I guess we don't know much about each other."

Collin put his hand under Melody's chin. He looked at her with such loving eyes that she would have agreed to anything he asked.

"I know that I love you and you me. I know that we were put on this earth to be together. I don't mean to make you unhappy. Please understand that a man have the need to provide for his family. Please understand where I'm coming from. I want to put a roof over your head. This roof is not of my doing."

Melody was quiet for a while. She began eating her food...............

After they finished eating Collin helped Melody clean up.

"So where is this roof of yours?"

Collin looked at Melody. He smiled. He took Melody by the hand. "If you're ready we can go now."

"I'm ready."

Melody and Collin left the house and got into his car.....................

After forty-five minutes Collin and Melody pulled up to a beautiful old Victorian house. It had a wrap around porch. A swing hung from it. Collin picked Melody up and carried her up the stairs and into the house. Collin placed Melody down in the foyer. Melody looked around. On her left was the formal dinning room. To the right was a sunken living room. It had an open floor plan. Straight ahead was a large kitchen. Melody walked towards it. She loved the large island in the center of the kitchen. Melody loved the cabinetry and the amount of storage it provided. Collin took Melody's hand and led her upstairs. There were three bedrooms and one bathroom leading to the master suite. When she got to the master suite Melody looked in. It was large. It was nicely decorated, but Melody thought it could use a women's touch. Melody stepped into the room. She walked into the bathroom. It was large as well and again looked like a man's room. Melody liked the room and thought of how she could change some things to make it feminine without removing his presence.

"So what do you think?"

Melody walked over to Collin. She put her arms around his neck.

"I love your home. It's beautiful."

"It's our home. You can change it to your liking."

"Thank you. I was just thinking it needed a feminine touch."

"So do you think that you could be happy living here?"

"I can live anywhere with you and be happy. I love you."

"So when do we move in?"

Melody looked into his eyes.

"Tonight."

"Are you sure?"

"I told you that I love you. I don't want to take anything from you. I will be happy here with you. This will be my last home." Collin looked at Melody. Melody smiled. "Three's the charm."

Collin realized what Melody meant.

"Would you like to go back and get some clothes?"

"That's a good idea."

Collin and Melody left for her house. They were quiet. To break the silence Collin turned on music. They both sang along with the songs. Singing along with the songs broke the anxiety. Collin was feeling like he was taking Melody from her home. He reached out and held Melody's hand.

"Collin you think we should stop and get some boxes?"

"Maybe you can get a few things now and we can come back during the week, because I don't think that anything's open. Are you hungry?"

"Not very."

"Tell you what, while you grab a few things I'll call and order something for dinner and we can pick it up on the way home."

Melody thought to herself, "He's very comfortable with calling his home mine."

When they arrived at her house Melody took a good look at the outside. Collin parked the car. They got out and walked up to the door. Melody opened the door. Once in the house Melody went upstairs to her bedroom and Collin went into the living room. Melody looked around the room. She went into the closet and pulled out her luggage. Melody packed all of her lingerie and as many clothes and shoes that she could fit into the luggage. Collin came upstairs. He entered the room. He picked up the luggage and carried it out to the car. When he came back into the house Melody was on her way down the stairs carrying the last bag. Collin met her and took the bag.

"You ready?"

"Yes."

Melody closed the door and locked it. She got into the car. She leaned her head back and closed her eyes. Collin took hold of her hand. He held it until they arrived at the restaurant. Collin parked the car and then got out. He went into the restaurant.........................

When he returned he noticed Melody was asleep. He placed the food in the back seat and closed the car door as lightly as possible. Collin started the car up and proceeded to drive home. When he arrived home Collin took the food into the house. He then took the bags and placed them in the foyer. Collin returned to the car. He opened Melody's door. Collin went to pick her up and she woke up.

"Go back to sleep." Melody allowed Collin to pick her up. She rested her head on his shoulder. Collin carried Melody into the house and up to his master suite. He gently laid Melody down onto the bed. Melody adjusted herself on the bed.

"Sorry. I didn't realize that I was so tired."

"You have jet lag. Rest, I'll bring the food up to you."

"I need to rest right now. I'll come down later."

"Ok."

Collin kissed Melody gently on the lips. He left the room and went downstairs. Collin fixed himself a plate and went into the den. While he ate Collin went through his mail. When he was finished eating Collin layed his head back and drifted off to sleep. Melody awakened. She looked around the room. Melody realized where she was. Melody got up. She went into the bathroom. Melody went into the cabinets and found a face cloth. She washed her face. As she left the bathroom Melody glanced at her watch. It was seven o'clock. Melody couldn't believe that she had slept for two hours. She was still sleepy. Melody walked down the long hallway. She stopped in each room. Before Melody pass it she looked around the room and thought of what she would like to change. When she made it to the end of the hall Melody went downstairs. She looked in the kitchen. Melody liked the kitchen. She saw the food sitting on the stove. She looked in the cabinets to find a dish. When she found it Melody fixed herself a plate and put it in the microwave. When the food had finished warming up Melody took it out and went into the den. Collin was asleep. Melody sat in one of the loungers and ate her meal. She often looked at Collin watching the ease of his breathing. Melody wanted to snuggle up to him, but resisted because she didn't want to wake him up. When she had finished eating Melody took her plate and Collin's into the kitchen. She washed the dishes and then went back into the den. Collin was still asleep. Melody walked over to Collin and lightly kissed him on the lips. He stirred Melody moved back. Then she kissed him again. Collin opened his eyes. He looked up at Melody. He smiled and wrapped his arms around Melody's waist. He pulled her onto him. Melody sat on his lap.

"This feels good."

Collin put his hands under Melody's legs. He adjusted himself. Collin stood, lifting Melody into his arms. He walked over to the wall and turned the light off. He walked upstairs carrying Melody....

Melody and Collin returned to work. They often had lunch together.

While at work they were not able to spend much time together because of their clients. Melody always arrived home before Collin. Melody would prepare dinner for the two of them. On most nights Collin was home by eight. Melody had become accustomed to waiting for Collin. She enjoyed having dinner with her husband. There were nights when she had to eat alone. On those few occasions Melody familiarized herself with her new house. She moved some of the small items from her house. Melody arranged to have the house sold. She hired Davis to be her attorney. She felt inclined to give him the business. When Melody called Davis to inform him of such he was happy to hear from her. Melody could tell he was taken aback when she informed him that she had gotten married. He congratulated her. Davis asked if he knew the lucky guy. Melody told him it was Collin. Davis chuckled and then said, "I figured as much." Melody asked him why. Davis responded, "I knew that it was more than friendship. I could tell by his expression when I came onto you. That was not a friend's expression. It was a man in love." After Melody got off the phone she thought about all of the times that Collin had said that they were friends. She resolved that they had began as friends and some how it had progressed into something more.

A year had passed and Melody became concerned that she had not gotten pregnant. She made an appointment to go see her gynecologist. Melody did not share her concern with Collin. Melody choose to go to the doctor on one of Collin's late nights.

After work Melody went home showered and changed clothes. Melody left the house and headed to the doctor. She prayed on her way to the office.

When she arrived at the doctor's office Melody parked and then went in. She checked in with the receptionist. While she waited to be called Melody watched the television in the waiting area. The story that was showing made Melody uncomfortable. The show discussed women having problems conceiving. When Melody was called, she was relieved. She didn't want to hear anymore. Melody sat in the examining room. The nurse took Melody's vitals. When the doctor came in he asked Melody her reason for her visit into the office. Melody told him that she had been trying to get pregnant for a year, but was unsuccessful. The doctor checked Melody's vitals and then had blood work done. Melody was asked to void in a cup. She waited a few minutes and then the doctor came back into the room. The nurse came in shortly after the doctor. She handed him the results. The doctor read it. He looked at Melody.

"You say you haven't missed a period?"

"No. Last month it was short."

"What do you mean?"

"Two days. Why?"

"What about this month?"

"It's due Monday."

"Don't bet on it."

Melody looked at him curiously.

"I don't understand."

"Congratulation."

"Congratulation?"

"Yes. You're pregnant."

"I don't understand."

"You're going to have a baby."

"I understood what you said, "I just don't understand. When, how? I haven't missed a period."

"Sometimes women don't miss their monthly. Yours was irregular last month." The doctor examined Melody further. "You are two months."

Melody couldn't believe her ears. Melody hugged the doctor.

"Thank you."

"I want you to return in a month."

The doctor gave Melody a prescription for prenatal vitamins. She went directly to the pharmacy. After getting her vitamins Melody drove home. As soon as she got into the house Melody went into the kitchen. Melody was stun when she saw Collin sitting at the table.

"Hey where have you been?"

"I didn't realize it had gotten so late. Have you eaten?"

"Yes. I just finished. You worked late tonight?"

"No. I just came from the doctor."

Collin got up.

"Are you ok?"

"Yes I'm fine."

"What, you were just going for a check up?"

"No. I went because I was worried that I had not gotten pregnant."

"What did the doctor say?"

"He said that I'm two months pregnant."

Collin looked at her in disbelief and then he rushed over to Melody. He hugged Melody and then backed away. He got on his knees, placed his hand on her stomach and then looked up.

"Are you sure?"

"Yes."

"I love you." He put his lips to Melody's stomach.

"I love you too little one." Collin got up and hugged Melody again. "Have you eaten?"

"No. I went straight to the doctor's office and after leaving there I was too excited to think of food."

"Well sit down. I'm going to fix my beautiful wife and child something to eat."

Collin fixed a light plate. Melody hadn't realized that she was hungry. She ate all of it. When she was finished eating Collin took her plate and glass. He washed them and they walked up to their bedroom hand in hand. They undressed and then went to bed. Collin held Melody. Before falling asleep Collin said, "I love you."

The next morning the couple woke up. They dressed. Melody grabbed a piece of toast and told Collin that she would get something to eat at work. Collin made her promise. Melody went to the school cafeteria and got breakfast. She ate most of it, not so much because she was hungry, but because of the pregnancy. At lunch Collin was right on time. He had a bag in his hand.

"What's this?"

"Lunch?"

"You brought lunch?"

"Yes. I thought this would be more intimate."

The couple ate and talked about Melody's pregnancy. Melody was surprised to see how excited Collin was. She remembered Juan being excited, but it was different. Collin was more attentive.........................

When Melody was five months Collin went with Melody to her doctor visit. She smiled at Collin's expression when he heard the baby's heart beat and in seeing the baby on the sauna gram. The doctor asked if they wanted to know the baby's sex. The couple expressed that they wanted to be surprised............................

Collin accompanied Melody to her doctor visits for the remainder of her pregnancy. They also took Lamaze class. In Melody's seventh month she and Collin took one of the bedrooms and turned it into the baby's room. Melody's parents were thrilled about the baby and Melody's happiness. They were equally excited that they would have another grandchild.

Melody stopped working in her eighth month.

Lisa became her best friend and often visited and checked on Melody.

Melody's parents also visited Melody more often to keep her company while she waited to go into labor.

Melody purchased a few things for the baby, but resisted buying too much because she didn't know the sex of the baby.

In Melody's last month she became restless. She began walking at least a mile a day. Collin took paternity leave from his job to be with her. He walked with her and tried to keep her from going to far from their home in case she went into labor.................. The week that Melody was due she and Collin's got up and did their usual walk. Half way into the walk Melody felt pressure. She bent over and held her stomach. Collin got a worried look over his face.

"Are you alright?"

"I think I need to get back home."

As the couple turned and started walking back Melody felt pressure again and stopped. She rubbed her stomach and made a noise. Collin put his arm around her to help her walk. Just as they made it to their property Melody felt the pain again. Melody's car was closer so Collin helped her into it. He ran to his car to get her bag out of the back seat. Melody made a sound. He hurried to close the back door and then jumped into the driver's seat. He looked at Melody.

"My water just broke."

A horrified look came over Collin's face. Melody placed her hand on the side of Collin's face and then smoothed it over it. "Don't worry. I still have time before the baby will come."

Melody called the doctor and informed him that she was on her way to the hospital. The doctor told her that he would meet them there. Melody hung up. She closed her eyes and did the breathing that she had practiced in Lamaze class.........................

When they arrived at the hospital Collin pulled into emergency parking. He got out of the car and ran over to the passenger side of the car. Melody opened her door and Collin helped her out. He put his arm around her waist and helped Melody into the hospital. When they were seen one of the hospital staff grabbed a wheel chair and pushed it over to Melody. She was helped into the chair. Melody gave the staff her doctor's name. He was called. The doctor came in shortly after the call. Melody was examined. She was taken to the birthing room. As soon as Melody was brought into the birthing room her contractions became stronger. After two pushes the baby's head crowned. The doctor cleared it's airways and then he instructed Melody to push again. Melody pushed. The doctor looked up and said, "Congratulations you have a boy." He held the baby up and then passed him to the nurse. The nurse cleaned the baby and then brought him to Melody. Melody and Collin looked at the baby and then at each other. Melody saw pride in her husband's face. After a few minutes the nurse took the baby. Melody was taken to her room. When they got to her room and they were alone Collin kissed her.

"Wow."

"Do you know how happy you have made me?"

"I guess I do now."

"In the excitement I forgot to call your parents."

Collin took his cell phone out of his pocket and called his in-laws. He told them the exciting news. Melody smiled to herself. Hearing the joy in his voice brought such a fulfillment. She had never felt such joy. After Collin had talked with Melody's parents for a while he handed the phone to Melody. Melody took the phone. Her father was on the other end. He also sounded proud. While Melody was talking to her parents the baby was brought into the room. Collin met the nurse and picked up the baby. He began talking to his son. Melody watched Collin as he made silly faces and sounds. Melody's parents heard Collin and got off the phone.

After she hung up the phone Collin walked over to her with the baby. Collin handed the baby to Melody. She took her new born son and kissed him.........................

The next day Melody's parents came to the hospital. They were mesmerized by their grandson.

Several days after Melody was released from the hospital a surprised baby shower was thrown for Melody and Collin. Her mother organized the party. A few of Melody's old acquaintances were invited. Tina was there. She was happy to see her. Melody hadn't seen Tina since she had gotten injured. She often wondered, but with being married to Bill she dared not be away from home. Melody felt bad that she hadn't checked on her since her assault. They embraced. Melody and Tina caught up on their lives. Both women were happy to see each other. Throughout the day Melody felt as if she somehow had finally found the life that she was supposed to be living. The life that had been snatched away by Bill. Melody mingled with old and new acquaintances.

After the party Melody went to lay down. She was exhausted. Collin, helped her mother clean up the house. Her parents left after the house was cleaned....................

Collin and Melody returned to work after six months. Melody's mother was a home maker so she watched Jr. while the couple worked. Melody's parents were overjoyed with spending time with their grandson...................................

Collin continued to work the hours he had before Melody's pregnancy so there were two nights a week that she put Jr. to bed alone. When Collin would come in late he would always check on the baby.

Although he was tired from his long hours Collin and Melody made a point of sharing their work day before going to bed...

Six months later it was Christmas Eve. Melody gave Collin one additional gift. She informed Collin that she was pregnant again. Collin was thrilled.

On Christmas day Melody shared the news with her parents. They couldn't be happier...............

Melody's mother became ill when she was four months. Melody took time off to take care of her mother. Two months before Melody was due her mother was admitted into the hospital. Melody mother's pneumonia turned critical.

Melody worried and as a result her baby girl was born premature. To Melody and Collin's delight the baby was healthy. She was small, but all of her organs were developed. Melody was released from the hospital two weeks after her baby was born. Collin took a leave from work and kept Jr. Melody's father spent much of his time at the hospital. Melody worried about him. He looked tired and was noticeably thinner. Melody tried to get him to eat, often telling him that he had to stay strong for when his wife goes home. He didn't listen and as a result he was hospitalized for dehydration and malnutrition......................

Melody's father was released a week later along with their daughter. They named their daughter after Collin's mother, Ruth Ann. They insisted on her father coming home with them. They set him in one of the guest room. Temporarily Ruth shared a room with Jr. Melody and Collin had not fixed up a room for her.

While Melody nursed her father back to health, she and Collin redesigned one of the guest rooms. Collin took care of the children while Melody and her father visited her mother...........................

Several months went by and Melody's mother was taken off the critical list and placed as stable............................

Six months later they brought her mother home..............

Collin returned to work on a part time basis................

Melody resigned from her position...................

As time passed the family decided that her parents would continue to live with them. Her parents rented out their home. They refused to live with them without paying.

The couple added on to the home, giving Melody's parents their own living space. They lived there ten years together until Melody mother's death. Her father lived a year later and died a day to the date of his wife's death. Melody became depressed. She tried not to show her sadness but Ruth picked it up and refused to allow Melody to remain in this state. She at eleven years old comforted her mother. Everyday Ruth would tell Melody that she loved her and not to go away. Melody realized that she was hurting her family and had to snap out of it. She struggled to get up everyday. When the children were at school Melody went on walks often talking to God and all of the people she had lost. Collin made a point of continuing their lunch dates, but it was hard on him. Although he tried it was difficult for him to comfort her. He had never seen Melody so depressed.

One particular day Ruth came in from school and hugged her. She told her something that one of her teacher had said in class and it made Melody realize that she had a family and that they needed her. Melody was so surprised at Ruth's words that she made herself face the hurt.

Months went by and Collin could see the change in Melody. Collin was happy that he had gotten his wife back...............

Melody encouraged her children to be all that they could be. Jr. graduated high school and tried college, but realized that it didn't fit. Jr. found that he was more of a hands on type of person. He liked working with his hands and as a teenager liked fixing cars. He studied and became a mechanic. Melody and Collin later put up the money for him to open his own repair shop. Ruth became a Psychiatrist. She was gifted with the ability to read people. Ruth worked hard and on her thirtieth birthday Melody and Collin purchased a small building for her to open up a private practice.